TO AVOID FAINTING

KEEP REPEATING:

IT'S ONLY A MAGAZINE

. . . ONLY A MAGAZINE

. . . ONLY A MAGAZINE

. . . ONLY A MAGAZINE

. . . ONLY A MAGAZINE

PERPETUAL MOTION MACHINE PUBLISHING
Cibolo, Texas
www.DarkMoonDigest.com

Dark Moon Digest—Issue Forty-Five

ISBN: 978-1-943720-67-5

PMMP
dark moon

www.darkmoondigest.com
www.patreon.com/pmmpublishing
www.pmmpnews.com
darkmoonhorror@gmail.com

ARTWORK CREDITS

Table of Contents Artwork by Allen Koszowski
Cover and Interior Artwork by Lori Michelle

DARK MOON DIGEST

ISSUE #45

FICTION

NON-FICTION

DARK MOON DIGEST is published four times a year (January, April, July, and October) by Perpetual Motion Machine Publishing in print format as well as an e-magazine version.

All correspondence should be addressed (via e-mail) to the Editor-in-Chief at *DarkMoonHorror@gmail.com.*

Cost per issue for ***Dark Moon Digest*** is $7.95 for the print edition and $2.99 for the e-publication version which are available in Kindle and Nook formats.

Print editions are available from the publisher at **PerpetualPublishing.com** as well as major online bookstores including Amazon, Barnes & Noble, and many other book dealers. Bulk orders are available through the publisher.

Story submission must be made via Submittable at **https://darkmoon digest.submittable.com/submit** or following the links on our website **www.PerpetualPublishing.com** or blog, **www.DarkMoonDigest.com**. Make sure you follow the submission guidelines which can be found on Submittable. Failure to do so could result in your submission being rejected for consideration.

All submissions are read by a minimum of 3 editors, so please allow 90 to 120 days after submitting for response. We encourage simultaneous submissions as we understand the perspective from the writer's side. However, please withdraw your submission if your work is accepted elsewhere. Any submission questions can be directed to the Editor-in-Chief at *DarkMoonHorror@gmail.com.*

THANK YOU TO OUR SUPPORTERS ON PATREON.

A.J Spencer, "Barely Miners" beardless dwarf porn, Adam Rains, Adrian Shotbolt, Alex Ebenstein, Allison Henry-Plotts, Amanda Niehaus-Hard, Antony Klancar, Austin Martin, Ben Walker, Betty Rocksteady, Beverly, Bill Morrow, Bob, Bob Pottle, Brandon Petry, Brett Reistroffer, Brian Asman, Brian James Freeman, Brian K Hauser, Charlotte Platt, Chas Phx, Chris Baumgartner, Cindy Gunnin, Claudia J Parker, Cockroach Conservatory, Crystal Lake Publishing, Cut, Dai Baddley, Dan Howarth, Daniel Scamell, Dave, David Demchuk, David Thirteen, DeerNoises, Dream Static, Drew Purcell, Emma Williamson, Erin Murphy-Jay, Eve Harms, Franklin Charles Murdock, Gengar, George Daniel Lea, Grant Longstaff, Gregory A. Martin, Ian Muller, Ingrid Taylor, Jack Smiles, James (Tony) Evans, Jampersand, Jason Kawa, Jay Wilburn, Jennifer Dury, Jennifer McCarthy, Jessica Leonard, Jessica McHugh, John Foster, John Rockwell, Jose Triana, Joseph Zablocki, Keith Burton, Kev Harrison, Kevin Lovecraft, Kit Michael-Ryan, Lee Widener, Lou Columbus, Mark Jones, Mark Patterson, Matt Gamble, Matt Neil Hill, Matthew Booth, Matthew Brandenburg, Matthew Henshaw, Michael Louis Dixon, Michael O'Brien, Miguel_Myers_atx, Mistina Picciano, Myrmidon, Nichole Neely, Nick Petrou, Night Worms, Nikolas P. Robinson, Patrick Tumblety, Paul Ramage, PirateFrequencies, Rachel Cassidy, Randall Lee Lovejoy, Rebecca, Richard Martin, Richard Staving, Rob Gibbs, Roger Venable, S. Kay Nash, Scott Beggs, Shannan Ross, Shelby MacLeod, Sheri White, Sherry Solorio, Steve Ringman, Steven Campbell, Steven Schlozman, Stewie, This Is Horror, Thomas Joyce, Tim, Todd Keisling, Traci Kenworth, Tyler Cooper, Webberly Rattenkraft, Will Griskevich, William Hull, and Zachary Ashford.

Want your name added to this page and saved for eternity? Head on over to www.patreon.com/pmmpublishing and become a patron.

Congregation
WILLIAM H. WANDLESS

MY MAMAW, rest her soul, liked to say Cray had been touched by the hand of God, though she might have been the only one of my people who held to that particular opinion. Uncle Ambrose once pulled me aside and told me to stay away from that Fontenot boy because the Devil had his hooks in him. I reckon that was what most folks believed.

But until I'm in my rocking chair, looking out on the river and letting the sun seep into my old bones, I'll tell it slow and true and set the record straight for anyone who cares to listen. I know for a fact what got hold of Creighton Fontenot. I saw the scars myself.

I confess it always surprised me that folks didn't take a shining to Cray, at least not like I did. He was a handsome boy, tall and lean, sweet-natured and sweet-tempered. He was smart, too, and kindlier than most of his kin. Folk took to me, born in Boston and dropped down among them when I was already eight, like I was raised in the parish, but him they kept at arm's length. A name like his, attached to a heap of old money and a family that went back seven generations, should have put him on a good foot, but I suppose it didn't square up rightly with the boy they knew or with the patch of tales which had grown up around him. Maybe folks were a little superstitious, maybe a little afraid.

I was never scared of Cray, nor was I ever afraid when I was with him. He had a quiet way about him, and most everyone steered clear unless they had good reason to seek him out. People tried to stay on the right side of the Fontenots, of course, and Cray could scrap better than most anyone I knew. I reckon there were a few local boys who might've liked to try him, but their people taught them to think better of it. No one wanted their son to be the first to learn how far Cray's gators might go.

Folk who grow up in the bayou aren't as a rule afraid of gators—respectful, sure, but not often fearful. The big bulls will lay claim to a stretch of swamp, and the mommas will protect their eggs and their babies, but for the most part they're just scenery with teeth.

If a gator doesn't want a body to get any closer it'll rear up and hiss, let everyone know it's there. They want what most want: a little space, a little peace.

That wasn't the way with Cray's gators, and it was that strangeness that spooked most folks. Cray's gators didn't do what other gators did, and all the gators clove to Cray.

The first time I saw Cray I was about ten years old. My momma had made me put on a Sunday dress to visit with the Fontenots, and I wandered out to the backyard when the grown-ups were done fussing with me. I saw a boy two or three years older than me sitting out by the fringe of tall ryegrass meant to blunt the edge of the swamp, a scrawny, shirtless, suntanned boy bundling up some twigs with twine, his tongue sticking out between his teeth. With him were two good-sized gators, maybe eight feet apiece, cozied up right beside him and having themselves a bask.

I steered well clear, as you might imagine, and it was going on maybe three years before I laid eyes on him again. I didn't have much cause to mix with the Fontenots, and Cray kept to himself. But when Berenice LeBlanc had cause to holler, the whole neighborhood knew it, so the day a gator ambled up to get a better look at her yap-dog and muscled its way through her screen door, I nosed in with a handful of locals who'd come over to see what was what.

Berenice had managed to shut the gator up in her bedroom, and she sent Bobby Boniface running to fetch Cray. I had heard more about Cray's ways by then, and I figured he was just a fearless boy with a knack for handling. I'd seen a couple at work before—two men from the wildlife office in Thibodaux who'd been called down to deal with a gator that was poking around the parish library. The two of them together had just enough tricks to tire that one out. I don't know precisely what I expected to see that afternoon, but it sure wasn't what I saw.

Cray Fontenot, all of fifteen years old, showed up, waved us back, and made a beeline for the bedroom. The gator had been thrashing around, no doubt looking for a way out, but it went nice and quiet as soon as Cray started talking to it through the door. I don't know what Cray said or how he said it, but a minute later he let it loose and the pair of them walked down to the water's edge side by side, pretty as you please.

I was old enough by then to know a wonder when I'd seen one, so I made a proper nuisance of myself after that. Truth be told I don't think Cray knew what to make of me. He was kind and passing friendly, but I doubt he was used to getting much attention. Even his kin had made a point of turning a blind eye to his doings with the gators. I never sensed any meanness in it. Like most folks, I reckon they'd hoped for a son they could teach up to make something of himself, to carry on the family name, to do them credit. What they got instead was a boy with the kind of gift that can't be earned or bought or taught, a gift he had to live with, like it or not.

And it *was* a gift—fearful to some but a gift all the same—and one Cray loved. I never saw him so happy as when he was waist-deep in the swamp, romping with a young bull he had never laid eyes on before, or when he was sitting in the low grass, a brood of new-hatched babies chirping in his lap while their momma looked on. I saw plenty of gators up close when I spent time with Cray. He even introduced me the two that haunted the Fontenot place, ones I named Claude and Sylvie so I could set them apart from all the other gators that came to call. And let me tell you something: they have old eyes, wise eyes, eyes that take the measure of you and tell you exactly where you stand. When those eyes looked on me, I felt small and wanting, even a little ashamed, like they were searching for something worth finding but saw in me something to pity. Between Cray and the gators there was nothing but kinship, respect, and reverence. I'll always envy that.

By the time he was twenty, Cray was halfway famous, at least in our neck of the woods. It wasn't anything he'd looked for, but I suppose when every gator you come across treats you like a son or a brother, you're bound to turn some heads. I don't know that things could have turned out any different than they did, but when I feel extra lonesome, I like to imagine what might've happened if those TV people had approached Cray in some other way.

The way Cray told it a man from Atlanta showed up on his doorstep and made his play, talking real fast about how he wanted to make a show to "celebrate bayou culture." When he realized Cray wasn't dumb enough to take that bait, he set it out more honest: he wanted to focus on Cray and his gators but planned to round out the rest of an hour with "colorful characters" and "slices of bayou life." Cray still wouldn't bite. By the time Cray walked him to the door, the man from Atlanta was snarling and spitting, threatening to make a show that would play up every story about hicks in the sticks and would do for gators what *Jaws* had done for sharks. Cray didn't much care at the time, but say what you like, the man tried to make good on his word.

They started shooting the show that very spring, and the Atlanta man made a point of trying to get Cray's goat. They set up at the St. Cyr place, a cabin just nine miles west of where we lived. They sent the St. Cyr family packing and put out a call to cast locals for the new clan, picking whoever seemed readiest to act the fool. They called the worst of the lot "Crazy Cray" and made him the butt of the dumbest jokes they could come up with. The stars of the show were Remy and Zeph, the one from Biloxi and the other from Shreveport, two handsome boys who would play gator experts on camera and pose as the proprietors of the gator farm they were setting up special for the show just next door. But the real prize behind the scenes was Sebastien Theriot, six feet of meanness and a known poacher. He knew his way around a gator, though, and he had their farm stocked *tout de suite*.

On the face of it *Bayou Born and Bred* looked to be more of the same as far as those shows go. Remy and Zeph would set out into the swamp, teach the audience a little bit about the habitat, come back home to the Triple-B Alligator Farm, and put on a show handling gators which had been raised up on a farm in Leeville and didn't have a lick of fight in them. That took all of twenty minutes, and the rest of the show was nothing but the pranks of the patchwork clan they'd put together. It wasn't my cup of tea, but I suppose it would hit the spot if looking down on other folks makes you think better of yourself. The state made the TV people hire on watchers from the Louisiana Universities Marine Consortium to make sure the gators were seen to, so I figured it would be fairly harmless all told.

Before long, though, a girlfriend of mine on the LUMC told me they had two problems brewing. The first was Theriot, who was up to his old tricks. Twice wildlife officers had been by the Triple-B to question him on account of gators that had turned up with their heads and tails lopped off—the plainest sign of poaching there is. The other was the plan for the finale, which must have been what the Atlanta man meant when he told Cray he'd try his best to make folks afraid of gators. To set up the next season the TV people intended to give anyone who cared to watch a sight to see: they were going to send Remy and Zeph after the Deacon.

That name doesn't mean much to most folk outside the bayou, but everyone between Lost Lake and Devils Bay has heard tell of the Deacon. It's a tale that gets passed along right around the time a boy has figured out how to row a pirogue and has one eye fixed on the line where the river water goes to salt. If you're fool enough to set out south at nightfall from one of the islands at the edge of the Gulf—Wine Island, Timbalier

Island, or the Isles Dernieres, depending on who's doing the telling—you might come upon the congregation, a great gathering of gators out in deep water where they oughtn't be. If you're fool enough to stow your oars and stay you might get to hear the Deacon preaching to his flock, but if you hear that sermon bellowed out you're never coming back.

It's the sort of tale that does what it's supposed to do, teaching boys with no sense to keep within bounds and mind their elders. The way my Uncle Ambrose tells it the Deacon learnt all the gators how to talk amongst themselves, and to hear three of them jawing brings bad luck because it means the Deacon will have to come to settle their dispute. My Mamaw says there's a single Deacon for every generation, and each of them will speak his piece only once, for it's a terrible thing to hear. And her mamaw told her somewhere past that string of islands there's a scrap of land you can't find on any map, and on that plot there's a chapel where a gray-haired minister lives and sees to the needs of the congregation during the long quiet when the Deacon won't speak. No matter who's telling the tale, though, all of them agree on one particular: the Deacon is bigger than any gator anyone has ever seen, twenty-odd feet if he's an inch.

At first I didn't think much of it. I've seen some of those sasquatch shows, and I figured they'd just use the same tricks to gin up a hunt—get a few close-ups of a big bull, let Remy and Zeph talk up the danger, close on a sunset, and call it good. I told Cray what they were up to in late April, and it didn't seem to faze him. Once summer had settled in, though, my girlfriend told me Theriot had bent the ear of the Atlanta man and convinced him to go for broke to make it look real. They'd gotten permission to set out from the Wine Island refuge, and Theriot would bring along a .458 Winchester rifle on the off chance they needed to take down something big. Remy and Zeph were none too keen on the prospect, but by the time Theriot was done, the Atlanta man wouldn't settle for anything less.

I told Cray about it; I thought we'd have a laugh. But he went all quiet and asked me when they planned to shoot the show. I told him I didn't know. Then I asked him if there was such a thing as the Deacon. He didn't answer.

We drove to the St. Cyr place that very afternoon to see if we could find out when they meant to tape the finale. I went to talk with the cashier at the gift shop inside the farm, and Cray went to the pen where they kept the gators. The lady gave me a small range of dates; the whole crew would head out the following week on a day when the weather was fair. I went outside to pass word along to Cray, but when I stepped out the door a janitor held me back, put a finger to his lips, and pointed.

Cray was standing at the far corner of the pen, bowed over the railing a few feet back from the chain-link fence that hemmed the gators in. Every gator in the place had crowded into that corner, the young ones chirping and the old ones croaking pitifully, all of them begging for his attention like pups at the pound. When Cray pushed himself away from the railing it looked like his heart was fit to break.

The next day Cray was gone. Berenice LeBlanc swore she'd seen him set out in a pirogue, and if that were true it meant he had a ways to go. Cray was the strongest swimmer I knew, and if he got gassed in the swamp, I'd never seen it. I passed by the Fontenot place a few times a day, checking out back to see if I could spot Cray relaxing with Sylvie and Claude. I saw Cray's momma fretting by the water's edge on the third day. We waved to one another but didn't trade a word.

On the fourth day Cray came home. I caught him splashing out of waist-deep water flanked by Claude and Sylvie, who looked to be propping him up. He stumbled through the fringe of ryegrass and fell down face first on the lawn. When I rolled him on his back I got a good look at the damage done—a ragged, livid dotted line across his chest, a matching line across his thighs just above his knees. Most of his wounds were deep bruises, thank God, because if the skin had broken, he'd have been done for. As it was there were good-sized cuts in the middle of the bruises just above his heart, and I could tell a couple ribs had given way.

Sylvie and Claude didn't fuss at all when I hauled him up to the house, but they made little whining sounds I had never heard a gator make before. I patched Cray up as best I could in the kitchen, got some food and drink in him, and hustled him up to his room. He was pale and shaky, and he looked so much like the scrawny, shirtless boy I first laid eyes on years ago that I had to blink it away. He dropped off to sleep as soon as I laid him down, and I sat by the side of his bed for an hour or two. I only left when his momma came home, and when I left by the patio door, I saw Sylvie and Claude, closer to the house than they had ever been before.

Cray called me the next day and told me what he had in mind. He sounded good, all things considered. He'd take two or three days to rest up, and then he'd set out for the Triple-B Farm. I told him I was coming, whether he liked it or not, and I asked him if I should try to rustle up some help. He told me no. "Help might come," he said, "but we oughtn't count on it."

I went over late that afternoon and found Cray out on the lawn with Sylvie and Claude. He was a long way from healed but looked better; he was already scarring, and his momma had changed his bandages and bound up his ribs pretty good. He sounded strong, resolved, and we put our heads together to work up a plan. When we were done there wasn't much to it: we'd head on over to the Triple-B after dark, Cray would cut the gators out of their pen, and then we'd set fire to the farm. We didn't know if that would put the show out of business, but it would at least hold up the finale, maybe make them think twice about sticking around.

We drove over on a Sunday night. The moon was big and full, so I rolled the last half mile without my headlights. We both kept real quiet, me with my eyes on the road and Cray looking out on the water.

I parked on a patch of dirt behind the production trucks at half past midnight, and we could tell right away that our plan would have to be scratched. The St. Cyr place was packed—it looked like the whole cast and crew was raising hell over there—and over at the farm I saw a flashlight play across the pavement by the gift shop. I looked to Cray, and we trimmed our plan down to the bone. I'd keep watch, he'd cut the gators loose, and we'd rendezvous at the car. That would have to do.

I found a good spot behind a big oak and kept an eye on Cray as he crept across the road and slipped into the water, a bolt cutter folded under his arm. Things went south and sour right after that. All the gators in the pen swarmed the spot where Cray was before he could cut a single link, and I could see the flashlight slashing quick from left to right, trying to see what they were up to. Worse yet, a truck rolled up and turned down the gravel track which led behind the farm. Someone was making a delivery, and the hour told me it was Theriot.

Cray had made it to the fence and started cutting, so I made my decision. I'd run up behind the truck and see if I could keep Theriot and whoever was patrolling the grounds on the far side of the farm, away from Cray. I started out real quiet but then got low and ran as fast as I could; the gators were making too much of a commotion for anyone to hear me.

The driver's side door of the truck was open, but Theriot was nowhere in sight. I climbed halfway inside and leaned on the horn. As soon as I did, I felt the truck rock, so I ran back to check the bed, knowing full well what I'd find. Theriot had three gators taped and trussed under a canvas topper, ready for the pen.

I can only give a rough account of what happened next. I grabbed a hunting knife from the passenger's seat of Theriot's truck, circled back to the bed, threw open the gate, and started cutting. I heard footsteps on the gravel behind me and a man's voice hollering. I heard a gunshot ring out on the far side of the farm. It's all a blur in my memory.

But some other parts I recall pretty well. Though I was afraid of getting bit, I remember the gators relaxing to let me get at the tape that held their jaws shut and pinned their claws to their bodies. I remember the way they looked at me, their eyes bright in the light of the moon. I remember a flickering of recognition, an old kinship.

And by God I remember that roar. Windows broke, and the truck shuddered. Bobby Boniface swore he heard it, and he was in Chocodrie, seven miles away. That roar nearly shook the soul right out of me.

The rest you can get from the internet. Whenever I start the story in my own leisurely way someone else will jump in and finish it for me, and those folks out on the message boards can spin a yarn better than I ever could. To hear them tell it, the network which aired *Bayou Born and Bred* wanted to stage a big publicity stunt to goose the ratings. They made up the story of a monster that cruised in from the Gulf, leveled the whole damned farm overnight, and brought the St. Cyr cabin down—pure Hollywood horseshit. Every member of the cast and crew was in on it and got paid to tell it just like that, even Crazy Cray, who supposedly got his legs pinned underneath a production truck and had to have them amputated. The show got canceled anyway.

They say there were sizable gator bites in the wood and big prints in the mud, but the bites would be easy to fake and no one took the time to cast the prints before it rained. Another cable network sent experts to the site to debunk the story a few weeks later, and they set the record straight: a gator that could make bites that wide and deep, the kind of bites that tore through timbers like cardboard, would have to be more than thirty feet long. There's obviously no such thing.

The only part of the story they couldn't square up quite as easy was what happened to Sebastien Theriot, who died from the bites of about twenty different gators, big and small. Pictures from the scene were leaked to the internet, and Theriot's face shows far more fear than you'd expect from a man who worked with gators all his life. Some believe he fell down drunk in the gator pen and the TV people made up the whole hoax to cover it up. They wanted to get the Atlanta man on camera to tell his side of the story, as he was meant to be at the St. Cyr place for a party that night to celebrate the show's renewal. Rumor has it he moved out to the desert, though, and no one's seen hide nor hair of him since.

As far as I'm concerned folks have a right to believe whatever they like. The only tale I can tell has a hole in it, so I reckon most of the others hold together better. I tried to fill in that hole, of course. I got myself a pirogue and rowed out south of Wine Island a few times to see what I could find. And every time I thought I spotted something—a shadow of a shack out there on the water, the flickering of a little cook-fire—a big bull gator nosed my boat around and turned me back.

I figure there'll be time enough for a proper telling later on. These days I like to spend my afternoons out behind the Fontenot place. Claude and Sylvie are getting on in years, but most sunny days they'll amble up from the swamp so we can have ourselves a bask. An old bull swims in to their waters now and again, but Claude and Sylvie never seem to mind. All three of them are content to set a spell and listen to me tell tales about a boy I once knew, a kindly, quiet, sweet-natured boy who grew up to lead a congregation. And when I'm done, that bull heads on back to deep water, taking a little of my loneliness with him.

William H. Wandless is a professor of English at Central Michigan University and a writer of poetry and speculative fiction. His latest stories appear in *Not One of Us*, *Dissections*, *Crow Toes Quarterly*, and *The Wondrous Real*.

THE SHED
AISLING CAMPBELL

THE SHED LOOMED, lit solely by the light from Mr and Mrs Khan's house next door.

Gabby fumbled with the sleeves of her dress, glancing at her brother, Scott, as he shone the torch on the shiny new latch and padlock. The key was clutched in his other fist. She looked back over her shoulder at the open kitchen door and her other brother, Jake, sitting on the steps watching them.

There was a click as the lock sprung open, followed by a clunk as Scott lifted up the latch and pulled back the door.

There was no creaking. Gabby felt like it should creak—big, spooky doors always creaked. But their father had been out last week and oiled all the hinges, so the door moved whisper-quiet.

'Go on then,' Scott said.

The shed stank of dust, of dirt and damp. The torch illuminated the floorboards, the handles of rakes, shovels and other tools stacked against the wall. Gabby's eye was drawn at once to the cotton candy clouds of spiderwebs gathered in the corners.

'She's not gonna do it, Scott. Let's just go play Fort—'

'No! I—I can.'

She forced her feet to move, one in front of the other, over the threshold and in.

'You won't lock it?' she asked Scott, wishing she had something to hold, to hug. She'd asked for a torch, her brothers had said no. She'd asked if she could bring Pebbles, her stuffed frog, and Jake had called her a baby.

'Well, how else are we s'posed to know if you stayed in there the whole time or not?' Scott said.

'But that's not—!'

Scott sighed, and she hated that sound. It was the sound of her getting kicked out, excluded—for being a girl, for being a baby, for telling Mummy. They'd only agreed to play with her this time because Daddy had told them to.

But Daddy had also told them to stay in the house until he got back.

'Just five minutes? And then I win?'

'Sure.'

The door swung shut in her face.

***

The darkness was unlike anything else Gabby had experienced in her short, electrically-lit life. In her bedroom at night, the streetlights were always leaking through the curtains, there was always the sliver of light from the hallway visible through her bedroom door.

Even when she closed her eyes tight the light still made it through—the darkness sometimes tinged red by the blood running through her eyelids, patterns like stars in a galaxy bursting behind them.

In the shed, the darkness was complete. There were no windows, just solid boards. If it had been day there might have been just a little seepage through the cracks under and around the doors, but it was seven-thirty in the evening and the sun had set.

Gabby's heart pounded. She'd forgotten to start counting. Five times to sixty, when the door would open.

She felt herself swaying, uncertain just where exactly she was in relation to walls, to tools, bicycle parts, and, most importantly, spider webs.

Someone laughed, the noise muffled by the boards. A distant door slammed shut.

Gabby wished she had chosen to sit down instead. It felt like she was standing on a tiny pillar, perched in the centre of a deep pit, and one tiny movement would see her tumbling down. She couldn't remember where the walls were, the door. Even the rough wood of the floorboards beneath her was obscured by the soles of her trainers. Her knees began to shake.

***

No one would describe Gabby as an especially imaginative child. She chose colouring books over the freedom of a blank piece of paper every time, and she always coloured inside the lines. Skies were blue, grass green. Skin was peach or brown.

There was no imaginary friend to share tea parties with, to build castles in the sky with. And while she loved her stuffed toys, and named every one, she didn't talk to them like they were real.

She'd tried once. Just once.

It had been while her mummy was staying with Nana and Grandpa again, and there was no one to play with or to read stories to her at bedtime and pick out what she was going to wear the next day. Her brothers had taken one of her toys—a Barbie she'd gotten last Christmas—and burned it with a lighter out on the patio. Dad had shouted at them, but then he'd shouted at Gabby as well. No one hugged her or told her that her brothers had been bad and mean and it was okay to cry. Instead her dad had thrust the partially melted doll at her. 'I'm not buying you a new one. Here, take it,' he'd shouted and then he'd grabbed her arm and forced the doll into her hand, squeezing hard when Gabby screamed and tried to pull away.

Back in her room, Gabby had looked down at her doll. She hadn't really understood the significance of where they'd focused their efforts—the face, the crotch—but it made her skin creep, her stomach twist like it was full of worms. They'd melted away the smile, the eyes, leaving only a scarred mass of pink plastic. Gabby had run her fingertips over the whorls and ridges. She'd tried to make her walk, but the hip joints were fused now. Gabby had stuffed the mutilated doll in a drawer and curled up on her bed with Sandy, her favourite stuffed toy back then, clutched close to her chest.

She'd told Sandy all about how much she missed her mummy, how she wished she would take Gabby with her when she went to Nana and Grandpa's house. How she wanted her brothers to stop being mean to her, for Daddy not to yell so much.

She'd hoped for something, a voice in her head which was on her side. When nothing happened, she'd burst into tears all over again, her face pressed into the fake fur of Sandy's belly, squeezing her tight in both anger and need.

So, as she stood swaying in the darkness, Gabby didn't imagine monsters hiding in the corners, stretching out towards her. There were no vampires, no ogres. Not even masked killers like in the nasty films Scott watched on his laptop. Gabby had told on him, after he made her watch a bit. She hadn't been able to sleep and when Mummy had asked why she'd told her everything. Mummy had gotten this strange look on her face, and then after she had left there'd been shouting. Mummy and Daddy. Scott and Mummy. Daddy and Scott. She wished she hadn't told, curled up with the covers over her head. And Scott had gotten her back the next time their mum was away. She'd gone into her room and found Sandy in pieces, ripped up and shredded with the head gone, so Mummy couldn't stitch her back together. The pieces had gone deep down in the drawer with the disfigured Barbie and Pebbles became her new favourite.

Gabby wrapped her arms now around her middle and tried to count at last. One to sixty five times. Even less now, because she hadn't started right away.

One to sixty.

Her heart rate began to slow again as the numbers passed through her head. She swayed backwards, unmoored in the dark, and her foot struck something. The something toppled and hit another something, and that other something hit a shelf. Metal clanged and the floor of the shed vibrated with the force of a hundred tiny objects falling. The sound swallowed her up, forcing out air and conscious thought as she waited for someone to come and shout at her.

She hugged herself, biting at her hand when the panic wouldn't go away, tears welling up. She kept seeing her father's face with teeth bared, hearing the way his voice would go whisper-soft so you could hardly hear him and then ratcheting up to full volume so loud your ears hurt and you couldn't help but flinch.

Her brothers would blame her, even though it'd been their game, their idea. And Dad had been the one who'd told them to play with her in the first place. It wasn't her fault they'd twisted the rules.

Gabby's bum hit the rough wood floor as she folded up, her knees tucked tight to her chest. She couldn't be crying when they came back for her. They'd think she'd been scared of the dark—like a baby, like a *girl*.

She rocked back and forwards, just small movements, but it helped.

And then, when the echoes had faded, there was the thud.

***

Gabby stared ahead into the darkness, where the noise had come from.

'Scott?'

Maybe her brothers had come back to try and scare her, by banging on the sides of the shed. She listened carefully, for the sounds of their feet, for their laughter.

There was another thud, a noise like scraping wood, and with it another sound which made Gabby cover her ears and rock faster.

It was high pitched, vague and formless, and it made the hairs on her arm stand up straight as posts. There was something familiar about it, but in the darkness, it sounded inhuman, ghoulish.

Gabby began to hum, and the thing in the shed with her made more noises. More bangs, more scufflings. It sounded angry, trapped in a rage. Thuds like a head hitting the wall in another room. Bangs like someone pounding on a door, like fists slamming into plaster.

She pressed her hands even tighter over her ears.

Scott and Jake played pranks all the time. Mean ones. Just like this.

She slowed down her rocking, took deep breaths. Five minutes must have passed by now, surely. It had to be them out there, trying to make her scream so they could win.

It was only a prank.

She clamped her hands down tighter still.

They'd have to let her out before Daddy came home. He'd know she couldn't have locked herself in.

They had to let her out. She'd won their game.

***

When the door to the shed finally opened it wasn't Scott or Jake. Instead Gabby looked up to find her father silhouetted in the shed doorway. No vampires. No ogres. Just him.

As he dragged her from the shed, Gabby caught a glimpse of the space where the noises had come from.

In the gloom of the shed she made out a wooden box, big, all wrapped around with ropes and chains. It wasn't making noise anymore.

***

By the time he'd got her inside, Scott and Jake were nowhere to be seen. It didn't matter about the door only locking from the outside. Didn't matter that it was their game. Daddy didn't care about that.

***

'That looks very sore, Gabriella. Can I take a look?'

Gabby glanced at Miss Everrett, the school nurse, as the nice lady kneeled down in front of her. Miss Everett nodded her head and smiled, so Gabby showed her.

'That's a very nasty-looking burn, isn't it? Can you tell me how you got it?'

Gabby swallowed. Her heart thudded in her throat. She opened her mouth, the sour tasting lie there, ready.

But what came out was 'Daddy held my arm over the stove. Because I went in the shed. There was a box that made really creepy noises . . . '

***

'It's all right, Gabby love. You just tell the detectives what you told the social worker—what you told me.'

Nana's arms were around Gabby's waist, hugging her close. Nana's lap was all boney, but Gabby didn't mind.

'Scott says it's my fault—'

'No, no. Gabby. Nevermind about your brothers, it's . . . important that you tell the truth now. You're not going to be in trouble. Understand?'

Gabby nodded.

'Can you tell me everything you remember about the box in the shed, Gabby? What colour it was? How big itt was?' one of the detectives said.

Gabby nodded again, a big one.

'Uh-huh. I'm keeping it all remembered so I can tell Mummy all about it when she comes home.'

Nana's fingers dug in and she pulled Gabby tight, making a strange noise in Gabby's ear. Like the thing in the shed which wasn't a ghost—because ghosts weren't real. When Gabby turned her face, she felt the warm wet of tears.

'Nana, why are you crying?'

But Nana wouldn't tell her.

Aisling Campbell is a British writer from a seaside town in southern England. Her work has appeared in the anthologies *C is for Cannibals* and *It Calls From The Doors*, as well as on The Dread Machine website.

The Author's Alley
Don't just create a book, create a work of art
Editing • Publishing • Covers
Formatting (print and ebook)
Bookmarks • Business cards
www.TheAuthorsAlley.com
Mention this ad for 25% any service *
cannot be used toward the printing of business cards or bookmarks

HERE THERE BE
MONSTERS
NIKOLAS P. ROBINSON

FOR YEARS SHE lived alone, a simple life in a simple stilted home nestled back from the apogee of a beautiful cove, between the tranquil beach and the lush, green mountains that hid her private paradise from the rest of the island.

During the height of the tourist season, she wasn't always so alone as strangers in kayaks and canoes discovered her sheltered beach. They treated her home with respect and, though she preferred a life of solitude, she often enjoyed the company and the stories they brought with them of life outside of her haven.

It was during one of these seasons when a lone visitor found his way to her peaceful pool. He caught her eye and there was something about him that drew her attention and held it. She caught his eye as well, and though he left before the tide went out without saying a word, he returned the following day and then the next.

On the third day, he didn't retreat with the receding tide and as night approached, he started a small fire with driftwood just beyond the water's reach. Curious, she joined him and they sat in silence together until the rising waters threatened to extinguish the flames.

With sadness, she watched him return to the water and retreat from view, her thoughts returning to the strange man all through the day, wondering when he might next return. As she drifted off to sleep, she wondered if she would see him again and hoped that she would.

She needn't have worried, as he was back again only half a day later, and during this visit, they talked.

They talked for hours.

They talked about many things.

Together they made a fire as night approached and they continued to talk until they were both exhausted. They slept that night on the sand, under the stars and in the dark they dreamed of nothing more than remaining just as they were.

With sunrise painting the sky above them, they made love on the beach as the rising tide lapped at their bodies.

When he left next, he assured her that he would soon return, and so he did.

This time he returned to stay.

There they remained together, living their simple life as one in their simple home tucked into the greenery of their secluded cove for the following years.

There was happiness and contentment for both of them there.

On good days they would swim together past where the shore pinched together, creating the shelter of their perfect home, the water becoming dark beneath them as the island shelf gave way to the depths.

The years were good to them and their love was strong.

They woke one night to a rumbling in the earth, a deep growling vibration that they could feel and hear, and both were afraid a tsunami might come, but the waves simply became heavier for a while and peace returned.

***

The sting which had started the end of it all seemed so innocuous at first, just a tiny bite from some insect or creature hidden in the sand. These things happened all the time, and neither of them had thought anything of it when it happened.

It was only after he'd started getting sick that they began noticing the shapes undulating beneath the surface of the water as day turned to night, hulking shapes, unlike anything they'd ever seen out beyond where their cove ended and the ocean began.

Soon the fish began to float to shore, collecting on the sand at low-tide when the water went back out, displaying marks of suckers and teeth that matched none of the deep ocean predators they knew inhabited the waves.

Larger creatures too washed up, smaller sharks and things that were rendered unrecognizable from the damage done to them.

Soon he was unable to join her as she attempted to clean their beach of the carrion washing ashore, his skin cracking and seeping in the sun, his stomach turning and unable to hold down anything she might prepare.

She tended to him as best she could, but neither of them knew what he needed and in their isolation, it would be weeks before a doctor could arrive on the island. Deep inside they both understood he wouldn't live to see the doctor.

Unable to breathe without difficulty, knowing that the end was near, he asked her to help him to the edge of the water where they might watch the sunset together one last time. The struggle in getting him to the place where the gentle waves lapped up on the shore was almost too great to get him seated before the sun reached the horizon, but just as the sky and sparse clouds ignited with brilliant colors, his feet slipped beneath the surface and he fell heavily into the cushioning sand.

Hand-in-hand they watched as the sun disappeared and the first twinkling points of light sparkled in the night sky.

The pain was fading and he knew it was time to go, but as he slipped himself with her help, into the water, the wounds on his flesh began to burn differently. The salt, he assumed, was adding its own bite.

He took in one last breath of the ocean-tinged air, holding it within his agonized lungs, looking up at her sadly smiling face once more before he let his head slip beneath the water.

With one last gentle shove, she pushed him away from the sand and to where the current might propel him out to sea.

***

Alone in their home, she continued to monitor the new shapes in the waters, surely some creatures stirred up from the depths and exploring the surface for perhaps the first time. She found herself scared, but filled with excitement at the same time, experiencing the thrill of something strange and new that hadn't yet become terrifying.

Only after she awakened one night to a racket caused by a solitary tentacle, slithering its way onto her patio, blindly seeking her out, did she finally feel true fear of what might be out there.

She beat at it with an oar and it snaked its way back into the depths, rejoining the writhing mass of tendrils she imagined it must belong to. Her safe, comforting home now host to strange new creatures which threatened her.

The tourists who visited her island became more infrequent as people began to disappear and rumors began to circulate about unholy abominations which swept the unwary away if they dared to wade out too far.

For months she lived like this, in new isolation, fearing that soon she must give up the home she cherished so much. Weary from remaining vigilant so late into the nights, she was too exhausted as the sun dipped below the horizon to notice the horrible eyes peering at her above the water and the way the waves were disrupted as with something skimming along beneath the surface.

She did not notice the threat until the pallid, swollen limb had wrapped itself around her waist and pulled her violently towards the water. As her head was battered against the sand, she saw sparks before her eyes and she felt only confusion and terror.

Then suddenly, just as quickly, the cadaverous tentacle released its tight hold on her and the momentum of being dragged to the sea was gone.

She collected herself and stood, her feet in the water, and she felt as much as heard an anguished roar from somewhere in the darkness that'd then fallen. Resigned and no longer afraid, she stood firm for a moment before venturing further into the welcome embrace of the ocean, standing with her waist submerged, her hands pushed and pulled by the movements of tiny currents.

Something broke the surface before her before slipping beneath the water again, too far away to make out anything in the dark beyond only the simplest details.

Still, she stood to face what came.

Though she couldn't see what lurked before her, she could feel its presence obstructing the water the way a person can feel someone moving silently in the darkness in the way they alter the flow of air.

Unafraid, ready to embrace what came, she reached out slowly with her hand, leaning forward at the hip just slightly, until her fingertips lightly brushed against something hard but flexible.

She flinched briefly but didn't pull her hand back, nothing attacking her just yet.

She laid her palm flat against the invisible form hidden by the water and the night and she followed by laying her other palm on the shape as well.

The unreality of it all slowed her response, the connections slow to be made in her tired mind, but she recognized the pattern in the ridge or scale beneath her left palm. She had rested her hand against that same cracked pattern for days just months before.

She began to slide her hands gently along the surface of the creature before her, feeling the same familiar pattern taking shape.

Awareness struck her like a sudden shock and she attempted to leap backward, her feet lifting from the floor of sand and she toppled back.

The creature sped forward, massive fins breaking the surface of the water as it beached itself attempting to catch her before she fell.

Eyes adjusted to the darkness, the moon peeking out from the clouds, she saw something that was at once alien yet familiar. Perhaps it might once have had the form of a man, but only in vestigial elements was that apparent. The scales though, the scales were the same pattern she came to know so well as she despaired that the man she loved was dying.

How could this be?

She asked the question aloud, timidly uttering the name of a man she'd loved so long that it felt like her whole life and the organism propping her up vibrated in a way she could only interpret as affirmation.

She began to cry and pushed herself away from the creature, retreating from the water and falling heavily against the sand.

The thing in the water didn't follow, but it didn't retreat from her either.

Finally, her mind reeling, she retreated to her home and she sleept in the bed that felt painfully empty, worse than it had for weeks.

The next night, as the sun set, the thing approached again. She watched it and returned indoors. The next four evenings were the same routine.

On the sixth night, while staring into the darkness, she heard a crash as of something mighty breaching the surface of the water far offshore. In only a moment, the shape she's been monitoring turned and sped away beneath the water, fins like razors slipping beneath the waves as it approached the deeper waters.

Moments passed and, though only faintly, she heard the sounds of thrashing in the distance.

There was silence for a while and then a screeching eruption that led her to cover her ears, the pitch like some unholy chorus rising into the night sky and shattering the peace.

Minutes later the familiar shape returned to where it was, floating vigil with her, watching her, she knew, though she could see no eyes.

It took her weeks of this, the same routine repeated, the creature from the shallows racing away when anything else rose from the ocean depths before she accepted the reality that seemed too profoundly unreal, too painful and mad.

The man she loves had returned to her, though his form was nothing she understood, and he was trying to show her that she was not alone.

She tentatively waded into the waters, her eyes closed, fearful that she had lost her mind.

It slid through the water and ran its scaled flesh against her outstretched hands and nudged her with what she assumes must be its head, unseen in the inky, impenetrable darkness of the night ocean.

***

Nourished by the meat of unearthly creatures clawing their way up from the depths of the cold ocean, he grew strong and his jaws powerful. The flesh of those unhallowed beasts shaped him into a monster himself, as he prowled just beyond the cove to protect his love in her home where she remained, watching the waters under the moonlight for those times when his massive fins broke the surface, assuring her that he was still there.

Nothing of the man he once was remained of his form, but within that sleek, aquatic killer he was still the man who had loved her so intensely while he walked upon the sand with her hand in his.

The transformation he'd undergone had not managed to diminish the heart and mind of the man he used to be.

Nikolas lives in the Black Hills of South Dakota, with his girlfriend, daughter, and three dogs. When he isn't writing, he produces the morning newscast for KOTA TV. His next novel is coming in 2022 from Madness Heart Press. You can find him on all social media platforms as @MeltdownMessiah.

"A METAPHYSICAL SCIENCE FICTION SLASHER THAT DOESN'T SCRIMP ON THE GORE"
—STEPHEN GRAHAM JONES, AUTHOR OF MONGRELS AND THE ONLY GOOD INDIANS
NOW AVAILABLE
www.perpetualpublishing.com
STANDALONE
PAUL MICHAEL ANDERSON

AVAILABLE
NOVEMBER 16, 2021
BENEATH
THE
SALTON
SEA
If you knew this
was the last
thing I'd ever
tell you, what
would you want
me to say?
MICHAEL PAUL GONZALEZ

TIM KANE
BREATHING SPACE

UNFAMILIAR PUDDLES OF light lurked in the crevices like cancer. Cate entered the vault—an island nestled deep within the ship. It was designed to protect her, though she felt anything but safe inside the place.

Cate pulled her legs through the slender conduit tethering the vault to the rest of the vessel. Her pulse throbbed as she eyed the lighted screen on the far side. Pushing off, she sailed through the circular room, the curved walls giving the illusion of depth.

Reaching the screen, Cate tried to bring up the vault's diagnostics, but her finger slipped and directed the computer to System Sealing. The flashing icon showed an animated display of a door shutting. She attacked the cancel button, pushing it three times before the screen cleared.

"Relax."

Cate tapped the button that brought up System Diagnostics. Categories and numbers filled the screen: temperature, air mixture, pressure, illumination. The vault's computer systems operated separately from the rest of the ship for a reason. In the event of a radiation spike, the inhabitants could rely on protected life support. But this meant that someone had to come in here from time to time to make sure everything stayed within nominal levels. Today, that someone was Cate.

Her gaze trespassed onto the wall and soon she became lost in the ambient glow of the room. The engineers who had designed the vault intended the milky pulse of light to soothe occupants, yet to Cate, it felt hollow.

She shook her head and directed her attention back to the monitor.

"Let's get this over with."

She skimmed through the remaining items. All checked within admissible levels. Touching the 'Maintenance Sign Out' button brought up a verification prompt. The system waited for her response.

"Cate Stockhart."

The screen confirmed her entry and then flashed to ready position.

She urged herself to go, but hesitated. A sick sensation curdled in her stomach. Cate shut her eyes and envisioned spinning around, heading for the conduit leading out of this room. Gripping the edge of the screen, she rotated her body. The fluid in her sinuses sloshed – a sensation akin to inflating a balloon in one's head. She opened her eyes. The hatch to the conduit lay directly before her.

Pushing off, Cate fixed her gaze on the murky circle. Two meters. One meter. She clutched the rim. Feet went first. The rest of her followed, propelled by the push she'd given against the hatch. The conduit pressed against her body, a tight fit. It had to be. The tube was pressurized against a sea of liquid hydrogen surrounding it. This fuel, along with an outer shell of tungsten and lithium hydride, protected the vault from radiation and solar flares.

She wriggled through the last few meters, finally shooting out into the corridor. She wouldn't look back at the aperture. Keeping her gaze on the intercom, she pressed talk.

"It's done."

There was a moment's pause. Had Faith heard her?

Then the intercom buzzed. "I love you."

"Then you do it next time." Cate ended the call.

The rungs in the corridor allowed her to glide toward the bow of the ship. At the end, she kicked off the floor and drifted into the cockpit. The walls, once a pristine white, had dulled to a grubby beige. Panel doors pockmarked the room. Some had torn loose over the years, revealing coiled tentacles of wire. Three viewports looked out onto the stars beyond.

Faith scooted up from her slouched position. She flashed that famous grin over her shoulder as if to say, "You didn't catch me." The glow of the instrument panel lit her face in alternating shades of amber and emerald.

"Glad you could make it," Faith said.

Cate ignored the comment. Faith only wanted a rise and Cate wouldn't give her the pleasure.

"Ready to get to some serious work?" Faith poked one finger at the viewport. The stars glistened like flecks of sand, but one grain sparkled intensely. "Another mucked up satellite, another dollar."

"And a million miles from nowhere." Cate pulled herself into the empty seat and latched herself in. "Let's get on with it." She tapped the buttons on the console, pulling up a read-out of their position.

Faith leaned back, flopping her head on one side. "Why do you hate me?"

"Oh shut up."

"We never talk anymore Catie." Faith gave a wry smile. "I spend all day piloting. The least I could get is a little attention from you."

"Here you go." Cate leaned over and socked her in the shoulder.

"Ow." Faith winced.

"Now suit up why don't you?"

Faith's smile broadened, creating tiny wrinkles at the corners of her cheeks. "Going in the vault bothers you."

Cate gazed at the controls, watching the kilometers tick down towards their target.

"Come on, just admit it," Faith pushed.

"No, it doesn't." Cate hammered her finger onto a button, switching displays.

"Then you take the walk."

Cate jerked her head up.

One corner of Faith's mouth hitched up in a smirk. "You go."

"Fine. At least it'll get done right." Cate unbuckled from the chair and started for the hatchway.

Faith caught her by the arm. "You don't have to prove anything."

Cate stared down, willing Faith to let her go.

"Peace." Faith took her hand away and held up a pair of fingers shaped like a V.

It never ended with that woman.

***

Cate slipped into a spacesuit and strapped on a thruster pack. The helmet's visor only allowed clear vision straight ahead, with almost nothing side to side. She had to rotate her whole body just to view the airlock hatch. She brought up her wrist keypad to eye level and pressed the button marked OPEN HATCH. The rush of her breathing filled the helmet.

Sunlight stormed the breached airlock, inundating the walls with a blistering temperature hike. The visor automatically darkened to an opaque black, a safety feature which allowed her to see only the barest outlines of the walls, now emblazoned white with sunlight. Faith had positioned the airlock door so that it faced the sun.

"Jesus," Cate muttered.

Faith's voice responded softly in the helmet. "Such the baby."

Cate didn't dignify this with a response.

She could lift the sun visor to see, but then she risked a face full of unfiltered solar radiation. Instead, she felt along the sides of the hatch until she found the rung. Gripping it, she swung herself outside and away from the light. Her visor stayed dark, stuck in protective mode.

"Come on you piece of junk." Cate slapped the side of the helmet. "Work." The haze lifted and her normal vision returned.

"Did you mean me?" Faith sounded hurt, though it was only an act.

"Yes."

Cate unraveled the tether from her belt and hooked on to the hull. Pulling to test the line, it felt secure. A keypad on her wrist gave access to the maneuvering thrusters. Keeping her back to the sun, she jetted around the hull and could just see the viewport. Faith waved from inside.

Cate scanned the stars. This far away from Earth, the constellations were still recognizable, but tweaked so they appeared strange and unnatural. When the ship left her field of vision, she felt as if she floated in a soup of stars.

"This is a whole lot of nowhere," Cate said under her breath.

"What?" Faith asked.

Cate located the satellite just left of the ship. "Found it. I'm heading over."

She puffed the suit's thrusters to close the distance. The satellite was a dinosaur. Butterfly panels, spread wide to collect sunlight, looked pitted with score marks. Crystals crowded the rump of the central cylinder and one positioning jet sprouted a cluster of icicles. She guided herself nearer, grabbing hold of the casing.

"What's the prognosis?" came Faith's voice.

"Don't know yet."

Cate grabbed the side and towed herself toward the iced jet. Lower on the hull the scoring worsened, lacerating the metal skin to reveal the satellite's innards. When she flicked on her suit lamps, the gouge glittered with encrusted crystals.

"Someone gave this baby a good punch in the gut." Cate circled to a nearby panel, which had lettering caked in grime. "Probably space debris."

Faith issued her typical prescription. "Slap on a bandage and get your butt back here."

Cate wiped one glove along the side, revealing the words *Propellant Tanks*. "It knocked into the fuel line."

No response from Faith. The one time she couldn't think of a proper comeback.

Cate gripped the panel door and yanked it open. Fragments of crystal broke loose and clinked against her visor, bouncing off harmlessly. Her suit lamps illuminated the interior. At the far end of the enclosure she spied the twinkle of stars—another puncture.

"Hey Faith, mind telling a girl what kind of explosives she's cozying up to here?"

Still no response.

Small etched letters ran up the side of the tank, coated in a film of dust and ice. Cate swept her glove across the writing. Grime hid in the recesses, still obscuring the words. Leaning closer, she tried to make out what it said.

"Cate." Faith sounded sober.

"Busy here." Cate scrubbed the letters with her gloved fingers. At the edge of her narrow vision, she noticed a pinpoint of gas escaping from the other canister. It could be the source of the cluster of crystals.

"Solar flare," Faith said.

Cate's hand petrified. "How long?" She tried to keep the tremor out of her voice.

"Space Agency pins it down as thirty-nine minutes." Faith laughed. "Why not just round it up to forty."

Because that extra minute would roast us, Cate thought.

She pulled her hand up. It seemed to swim in slow motion. She set the timer on the keypad for thirty-five minutes.

"It could be nothing," Faith continued. "Some probe closer in took a bath and they want to blame something."

The digits on her wrist screen flashed, counting down. When the timer read zero, Cate knew where she'd be, huddled inside the vault like a scared rodent.

"But, lets , , , you know," Faith said.

"Play it safe," Cate finished. Her heart thrummed in her chest. "I'll be there."

She gazed at the tank. The section she'd wiped clean showed tiny engraved lettering.

N - - R - CAC - D

That last one was obvious enough—Acid. Cate frowned, trying to recall all the various propellant combinations used by older satellites.

A flash of light caught the corner of her eye. Then everything went dark.

***

Cate knew her visor had fogged up because she couldn't see a thing. She hammered on the side, trying to get the helmet to relent. Her head responded with a dull ache.

"Faith?"

The radio emitted the gentle hiss of background radiation.

Instinctively she brought her wrist up to read the display, except she couldn't see a thing. Lame move. The visor in protective mode blotted out everything.

Her breathing accelerated, coming now in short bursts. At this rate, she'd burn through her air reserves.

"Calm down. Just work things through."

Something had set the visor off. Usually that meant direct sunlight, but she'd had her back to the sun while working on the satellite.

"So, if it wasn't solar radiation , , , " Cate let the thought dwindle down to nothing.

Her hand fumbled at the latch that would slide the protective visor up and release her from the blind prison. She hesitated. If she faced the light, the full force of the sun would pump the temperature up to two hundred and fifty Fahrenheit. Then she might truly be blind. Still her hand gripped the latch.

Maybe open it a crack, just to test things out. She could hold up her other hand and block most of the light. The whole idea was lunacy. She knew it. But she had to see. The darkness ate away at her sanity.

Holding one hand out to block whatever light came streaming in, Cate unlatched the sun visor. The curved window popped up, creating a crack in the shield. She cringed. When nothing happened, she opened her eyes, not even realizing in the dark that she'd closed them.

Through the breach, she glimpsed stars, a black sheet of velvet spread over so many pin pricks, but something didn't feel right. She pushed the visor all the way up and gazed at the celestial field. The stars swirled.

Her body spun at an erratic wobble, the sky before her zigzagging back and forth in a crazy merry-go-round. Any control she thought she had over her breathing slipped away as her lungs and heart conspired to bring her mind to a dead stop. Swaying shadows played over her outstretched arms, indicating the sun was behind her. At least she had that going for her.

Cate closed her eyes, now embracing the darkness she'd so desperately wanted to throw off.

"Please Mary, mother of God , , , " Her mind ran blank of the rest of the litany. She completed by adding a simple, "Help me."

Cate opened her eyes and stared at the timer on her wrist. The readout listed twenty-seven minutes and seventeen seconds. It was all she had. Her life was measured in those amber numbers ticking away, now only twenty-seven and ten.

Tears trickled down her cheeks.

"Stop that crying. Just quit it."

Her chest heaved under the burden of sobbing, but she forced her lungs to slow, until each breath became steady and controlled.

"That's right. Keep it together."

Bringing the keypad into view, the timer now read a little over twenty-five minutes. She ignored it and put her fingers on the controls. If she could stop herself from spinning, she might be able to spot the ship. She clung to this reasoning.

Even though her rotation seemed erratic, the stars straight ahead hardly moved at all, while those farther out rambled in circles. She cycled mostly counter-clockwise, with some wobble forwards and backwards. Cate gave the thrusters three short puffs and her spin slowed. Several more spurts and the stars settled into a calm portrait.

The tether dangled loose in front of her, torn in two. Seeing this almost sent her to the brink of tears again, but Cate held them off.

The ship was nowhere in sight.

She craned her head to the limits her helmet would allow, but only saw the speckle of stars. How did she get so far away? A sudden thought came to her, clearing away all others—the writing on the side of the fuel tank. She could see the outline of the letters clearly. Her mind filled in the blanks: NITRIC ACID. That meant the other tank must have been hydrazine. The two didn't need oxygen to combust, but combined, they packed a wallop. She counted herself lucky to have both arms and legs still attached.

Seven minutes. That's how long she'd been unconscious. It's also how long she'd drifted away from the ship. The suit's thrusting jets were designed for maneuvering, not distance. She might need every bit of the twenty-two minutes left just to reach the ship, assuming of course she choose the correct direction.

The explosion would have sent her backward, away from the *Bravo*. If she headed straight, it should bring her to the ship, and Faith. But the spin and wobble had thrown her senses all to hell. She put her fingers against the controls. The suit contained enough fuel for one concentrated burn.

Her hand hung over the keys as thoughts blitzkrieged through her brain.

Push it.

Don't. Wait for a recognizable star, something you missed.

Do it now!

No, Try a slow burn. Take more time ,,,

But Cate didn't have time.

Her finger pressed the button and the thrusters came on, full force. Her body slammed against the back of the suit. The tether, which had drifted lazily in front, whipped behind.

The fuel gauge ticked down. Five-percent. Three-percent.

She stopped the burn at one-percent. Enough left for perhaps two seconds of burn.

***

Sometime over the next fifteen minutes hope gave ground to pessimism.

The stars remained fixed and empty, the pulse of light millions of miles distant. Cate had picked the wrong direction. The *Bravo* lay somewhere behind her, speeding away with each second. She hardly had the fuel to stop her advance, much less reverse course. The flare would reach her, carrying skewers of radiation with it. Then she'd roast in her suit.

Her gaze wandered away from its dead-ahead stare and caught something just below and to the left. Not much, a winking star maybe, but it might be everything.

Cate puffed the jets a little to rotate, but it looked like another patch of open space, no different than the one she'd been staring at for the last fifteen minutes. Then it flashed again. It could be just a chunk of the satellite.

But maybe.

Cate drifted a least a thousand meters off course. Using the last of her fuel, she compensated by thrusting straight down. This corrected her bearing and the glimmering beacon centered in her sights.

As she drew closer, the tiny silhouette showed the *Bravo*. Her ship. Cate wanted to cry.

Yet as the seconds ticked by, and the ship grew more distinct, something felt off. Her trajectory was too high. She'd overshoot it. Probably by only a few meters.

Cate pressed repeatedly on the thruster buttons, but the propellant tanks were dry. The salvation of the *Bravo* grew both nearer and farther with each passing heartbeat. Panic crept up her spine, paralyzing muscles as it went. She urged herself to think, but she couldn't remove her gaze from the advancing ship.

Cate spotted the armature. The attenuated arm extended in a question mark, ready for a rescue. Faith must have brought it out.

Cate watched the pincers at one end. Her breathing came in ragged pants. Each breath lured the arm closer. It wasn't until she flew over the ship that she realized that the armature hadn't budged. She sailed right by, only meters away, more than close enough for it to reach out and grab her. It remained frozen like a deformed finger. Something had gone wrong. She didn't understand. Why would Faith bring the arm out and not activate it. Unless she'd already given up.

Cate glanced at her watch. A minute and five seconds left.

She spied the torn tether, one end still anchored to the airlock. Her last hope. It dangled twenty or thirty meters to her left. It might as well have been a million. She unbuckled the thruster pack and it drifted sluggishly. Cate snatched the pack before it slipped away. Even emptied of fuel, it felt massive. Holding on to the buckles, she bent down and put both feet on the pack.

Cate grunted and shoved against the load with her legs. It worked, her trajectory shifted toward the tether. She held her arms out, fingers splayed to their fullest extent.

The tether hovered a mere dozen meters away, its line frozen against the stars.

Closer. Her fingers stretched out.

The wrist alarm blared. Time was up.

The tether slipped through Cate's outstretched arms and slapped against her helmet. She fumbled as it slid along the length of her body. Her fingers caught hold of something. Her body flipped backward and the tether yanked free of her grasp.

It trailed through her fingers, the end threatening to disappear forever. She clamped down and squeezed. Another jerk at her shoulder, this time accompanied by a snap she could hear through the confines of the suit. Pain lanced through her shoulder.

Light streamed into her helmet. She faced the sun now. Furiously she groped at the outer visor, pulling it down and committing herself to blindness. In the dark her rapid breathing accelerated.

Faith had said thirty-nine minutes. Cate was positive. And she'd set her timer to thirty-five. That meant that there were still four minutes left.

She dragged her body down the long tether. The snap she'd heard was her shoulder dislocating. A jolt of pain jabbed at her with each pull, but she didn't dare let go. Both hands gripped the cord.

An object, then another, thunked against her suit. After a moment, a barrage of space debris banged against her, pieces of the satellite, now exploded into bits. She towed herself forward for what seemed like an eternity before her hand clunked against the metal of the ship. She rotated away from the sunlight and lifted the visor.

A blackened gash tore along the hull. A chunk of the satellite had punched through and the scoring stretched all the way to the cockpit.

She worked the hatch and pulled herself in. No point in pressurizing with the hull breached. She overrode the controls and cranked open the interior door. Cate tried using both hands, but her shoulder throbbed in agony. She worked the manual door crank with one hand.

No blast of air accompanied the open hatch. The life-support systems had been compromised. Computer screens embedded in the walls flickered sporadically, casting the halls in an artificial lightning storm.

Scorch marks spattered the corridor leading to the cockpit. Had the breach caught Faith unaware? Flames needed oxygen to burn, so she probably vented the ship's atmosphere herself, to choke the fire off. When the atmosphere surged out, Faith might have had enough time to get into the adjacent hall, and to a suit.

A chill flashed through Cate, leaving goose pimples along her skin.

Faith was alive. She had to be. She was holed up in the vault, ready to tease Cate about being late.

"I'm coming." Cate grabbed the rungs and sailed down the corridor.

Reached the hatch leading to the vault, she scrambled through the narrow conduit, emerging into the milky inner sanctum.

The room was empty. The walls glowed a pale white.

Where was Faith? She was supposed to be here.

The screen on the far wall already showed the first pings of radiation. The counter spiked erratically. If the conduit were not closed soon, radiation could funnel right into the vault.

Sweat trickled down Cate's face and she spun, sure that the sensation was radiation bombarding her skin. Her heart hammered in her chest.

She brought up the System Sealing protocol. A banner along the top of the screen continued to display the current saturation levels. The emissions had surpassed tolerance levels and threatened to short-out the vault's computer.

She poised one finger above the button that would seal the vault. Her gaze fixed on the darkened conduit. The light from the corridor beyond flickered. Could that shadow be Faith?

The screen next to her flashed orange. Cate glanced over: INTEGRITY COMPROMISED.

The gauge indicated lethal doses saturating the ship. The radiation was frying whatever computer systems were left. Her heart thumped inside her head. Nothing could live through that.

Sweat tricked around her eye and down her cheek.

Her mind seized.

Too late. The bombardment had reached her.

She glanced at the hatch once more. And Faith was there. In a suit and crawling down the conduit.

Cate yelled to hurry, but no sound penetrated the suit.

Faith saw her, a mix of joy and terror on her face.

The hatch doors were closing.

Looking back, Cate saw her finger touching the screen. She'd pressed the button.

Faith watched, her eyes screaming for more time. Just seconds.

Cate might have halted the sealing sequence or reached out to drag Faith through. She did none of these things.

Faith made a final lunge, but her hand fell short and the doors shut. She was gone.

With the hatch shut, the screen switched from its radiation gauge to measurements of life-support. Heat, pressure, and air came online. The walls around Cate pulsed with a soft nurturing glow.

She was protected from the radiation. She had preserved her life.

But that was all she had.

Tim Kane loves things that creep and crawl. His first published book is non-fiction, *The Changing Vampire of Film and Television*, tracing the history of vampires in television and movies. Published stories appear in *Exchange Students*, *Lovecraftia*, *Attack of the Killer*... and *ProleSCARYet*. Find out more at www.timkanebooks.com.

SOMETHING SINISTER IS HIDING IN THE SMALL TOWN OF PERCY, INDIANA...
TOUCH THE NIGHT
MAX BOOTH III

HAPPY
THOUGHTS
SAMUEL P. MCQUAIL

I CAN SEE THEM, you know. Every time I step into the street, I see the little black curls of smoke polluting everyone's minds. Squirming, floating, writhing their way through otherwise pristine thoughts. He worries about his loans. She fears for her mother's health. They try to choose between saving their crumbling relationship or finding another. Everything smoke touches turns a little darker until soon an entire lobe of grubby grey has blossomed into sight. I can't stand it. Who could? Knowing all the nasty things that make smiles droop and tears fall. I can't stand to see them suffer like that.

So, I pluck the smoke out.

It doesn't hurt. I would never do something if it really hurt. I just . . . reach forward with my mind and pull out the wispy worms before they can dig too deep. Sometimes they still leave a little grey behind, but it always clears. And then the smiles are back. Those big, beautiful grins I love so much. It only takes a few minutes, and it makes me so warm to help everyone in town.

I don't think they know. People love being around me. I used to think it might be because I take their bad thoughts away, that they were being selfish. I had to pluck that thought out of myself. How could I make anyone happy if I wasn't happy? And I am happy now. Very happy! And everyone loves being with me because I make them happy too. Isn't that what friends are for?

But . . .

Sometimes I find people who've caught on. Who know. New residents, out of town guests or those rare ones born with my gift. I can tell they're like me because their heads are full of nasty things. Less like smoke, and more like . . . oil. Thick and viscous with everyone's thoughts inside their head. I try my best to pick away at their troubles. To let them know it's okay to have a gift like this. That they *should* make people happy. But it's so hard with some of them.

They think the black smoke is important.

That people should worry and be afraid and it's wrong to never be sad.

It takes me a long time to pluck that feeling out of their heads. It's such a deep-seated, nasty little thought, isn't it? So insidious and corruptive. But it's okay. I understand how hard it is to get rid of something like that yourself. How it can infest everything until your brain is full to the brim. That's why I'm here. I help them to be happy, and to see why they need to make everyone else happy too. You understand that, right?

You're not like *her*, are you?

She was a nice young woman from many months ago. She had so many reasons to be happy. A loving girlfriend, a beautiful house, a nice job . . . But she wasn't. No, not at all. Her mind was ugly: filled with oily thoughts and wrong ideas. Ideas like how strange it was no one else in town had the same black smoke she'd seen before. She thought everyone was wrong. Thought we were all scary and strange. Us being happy made her unhappy. That wasn't so bad. I'd seen it before, you know. Gifted people are always scared of what I do when they find out. But I pluck away the fear and they become just as happy as me.

Not her. No.

It was bad enough she wasn't happy. Bad enough it took me days to wriggle through her mind and pull the darkness away, only to find an even blacker pitch inside. Imagine that; how truly, desperately unhappy did you have to be to hide it so? No, no, no. Bad enough one person in a hundred thinks such thoughts, but for her to *put those thoughts in others* . . .

Ahem, my apologies. Let me just . . . there we go. The anger is all gone now.

But you see how horrible it is? Even I became unhappy with her. Maurice was happy. He didn't *need* to mourn his wife anymore. And the Joneses . . . The stillbirth was so hard on them, I simply had to take that away. And let's not forget poor little Timmy being scared of his uncle. He's such a nice, happy man with good, happy thoughts. The boy needed to focus on the silver linings, you know? But not with her around. No, she just had to slip in all the negative thoughts. To make the Joneses cry, make Maurice lonely, make Timmy . . . it took me days to sort them all out again, let me tell you.

I couldn't stay quiet, I had to confront her. I had to! But she wouldn't listen. She knew what I could do, and she hated that I did it. I never found out why, you know. She was screaming such nonsense about right and wrong and freedom... honestly, she was too far gone. There was nothing but roiling pitch in her head. She couldn't see, no matter how hard I tried. I *do* free people. I free them from the nasty thoughts, from the burden of unpleasantness. I kept trying to pluck hers away, but more and more kept forming until everyone's eyes were on us, filling with the same insidious thoughts . . .

I made it quick. I really did.

It took me quite some time to clear away the thoughts she'd left behind. Little worms squirming inside the deepest reaches of everyone's minds. I understand. It wasn't something you *could* be happy about. Even I wasn't happy until I plucked the guilt from my head. But now I am, and so are they, and even though she was never happy, I do wish she could have been. If only she'd accepted me.

Oh dear, I've made a few little curls appear in your mind, haven't I? I suppose it is to be expected. All this talk of unhappiness. If you'll just let me reach inside for a moment . . . There. All better. Of course, you'd remember what I said. I never took that away. We remember everything. It'd be so cruel to take the memories away. And I'm not a cruel person.

I just want everyone to be happy, you see.

Sam McQuail is a British author with both a flair for the dramatic and a background in psychology, both of which see frequent use in his work. Best tempted to parties with the promise of cheesecake and cats.

Jurassichrist
Michael Allen Rose

20 Things I want to See in Horror Movies

20. A family goes about their normal morning routines. Ominous music plays over the top of everything. Brushing teeth. A close up of eggs cooking. A kid packing his bag for school. A weary wife packing sack lunches. Music cues hit every time one of them says something they plan to do that day. This goes on for an hour and fifteen minutes. The music builds as the father tells everyone goodbye, gets in his car, fumbles his keys, starts it, backs out, drives away, and fade to black. End of movie.

19. Every man in the movie is stark naked. The women are fully clothed. It's a psychological thriller where they are trying to track down a killer. No one references why the men are naked the entire movie.

18. A woman struggles to free herself from a Saint Andrews cross in a dark basement before her captors return. She finally gets one arm free, but the man is stalking down the stairs and approaches her. He lets her go, she pays him, they make an appointment for next Thursday, and they part ways.

17. A cell phone company hires a paranormal investigator to figure out why coverage fails when people are being chased by killers. It turns out there are not enough towers in rural areas.

16. An old man tries to get crows to leave his lawn. They are perched on every branch, wire, and fence. He tries everything to run them off. More and more birds join the growing murder. Finally, he makes peace with it, starts feeding them, and trains them to do tricks. This movie is to be shot in black and white with no dialogue and it lasts three hours and forty minutes.

15. Two brothers working as bathroom remodelers have a falling out over which way the door should open. After there is a terrible tragedy from a bathroom door that opens out, one brother goes on a killing spree to cover his tracks.

14. Two hours of reenacting the most iconic and gory scenes in horror history, but all with Muppets.

13. A slasher film, but with no final girl. The only survivors are the most toxic male characters and you're left disappointed the killer didn't do a better job.

12. An old man at the beginning of the film warns the characters not to go to the haunted cursed place. Half the group listens and goes somewhere else. The film follows those who left. They have a fun weekend with lots of character work and growth. They hear about the slayings secondhand through news broadcasts, phone alerts, and text messages from their friends they assume are all jokes.

11. Stephen King writes a *Friday the 13th* miniseries that matches the cinematic quality of the 1990s *It* miniseries. The film follows Jason from his perspective. There is a ton of exposition and flashbacks with very little actual slashing. The ending is rushed and unsatisfying.

10. While we're on Stephen King, I'd like to see a Quentin Tarantino directed double feature of *Desperation* and *The Regulators*. The actors from both films play the corresponding roles from each book even in cases where the ages of characters are drastically different.

9. A zombie movie where the characters are constantly running and fighting to survive. You see plenty of slaughter but never once see or hear a zombie on screen.

8. A closed room movie with a divorcing couple negotiating who gets what from their possessions. The couple, the lawyers, and a few other people are in the room. The first half of the movie is a drama involving shouting, yelling, and crying. When they start trying to split up the Beanie Babies, it turns bloody violent. No one can escape the room. The couple ends up the last two left. Even though they are mortally wounded, they have sex in the middle slaughter. The movie ends with their climaxes and deaths.

7. A remake of *Troll II*, but worse than the original.

6. A *Nightmare on Elm Street* film where Freddy attacks a school of method mimes. There is no dialogue as Freddy grows more and more frustrated at how well the mimes keep trapping him in a box in their dreams.

5. Weiner: A film about killer Dachshunds who develop a rabid hunger for human male genitalia. Women are split on whether to help or let it play out. Disgraced New York politician Anthony Weiner plays himself and is the hero of film who finally defeats the horde of rabid dogs with the help of the women he's been sexting. The final scene is him sacrificing himself to lead the dogs to their doom as they feast upon his manhood.

4. An adult film that is only available on Pornhub. It starts out as hardcore sex with no plot. After ten minutes, the story becomes more complex. By the twenty minute mark, it is a psychological thriller where the actresses are fighting for their lives. There is some nudity, but no sex. At the end of the film, the actresses and surviving actors get together to celebrate with one more orgy. It cuts to credits before the sex starts.

3. A killer stalks a horror convention slowly closing in on the writers. Most of the film is writers and fans complaining that horror movies don't scare them anymore, that there are too many remakes, that their own

books would make better films if Hollywood would just give them a chance, and there is nothing new or creative being done anymore. They are too drunk and involved in their debates to realize they are being killed one by one.

2. A psychiatrist wants to kill his mother, but she keeps evading him which drives him further and further into insanity. He finally gives up and starts jerking off to one of her pictures. She sneaks up behind him and strangles him with one of her stockings. The death scene takes 23 minutes.

1. A film based on *65 Stirrup Iron Road* including the meta portion where Jack Ketchum got tired of the other collaborative authors' nonsense and lost his shit on them and the entire extreme horror/splatterpunk scene and the other authors just went along with it because it was Jack Ketchum.

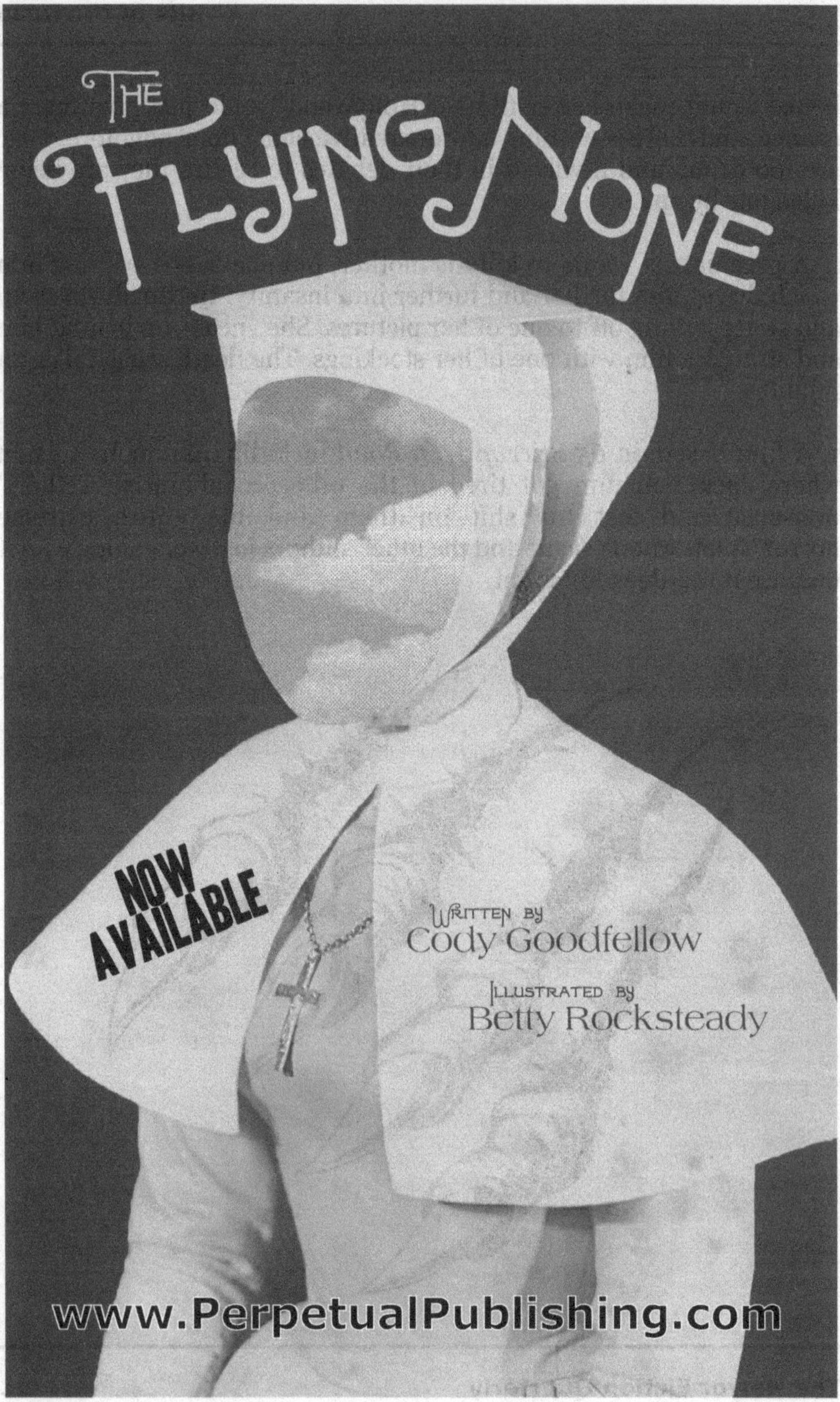

THE FLYING NONE
NOW AVAILABLE
Written by
Cody Goodfellow
Illustrated by
Betty Rocksteady
www.PerpetualPublishing.com

The Matters of Faith Podcast

MATTERS OF FAITH

PODCAST WITH JAY WILBURN

ESTD 2017

With your host
Jay Wilburn

on the
Project Entertainment
Network.

MAN OF THE HOUSE
JOSH TAYLOR

WHEN I WAS YOUNG, my father would sometimes roam the house on all fours like an animal. I'd put up my hand and scream, "No!" Sometimes he'd take me in his arms, apologize, and hug me until I stopped shaking. More often he'd pace right up to me, shoulders moving under his skin like a big cat, lips parted in a toothless grin.

I didn't have the words to explain it to my mother. "No go," I'd say. "No daddy dog."

She'd kneel down and hug me goodbye, relieved I was finally starting to talk. My father would just rub my head. He had early arthritis. I don't think my mother could imagine him on his hands and knees, gliding face first down the stairs, brushing past my leg, sniffing my hand. No, she didn't know until the day she came home to find the dog's throat ripped out. They went in their bedroom and shouted for a few minutes, and then spoke more calmly. I remember standing on my dresser, listening through the ceiling vent.

"So, the cat didn't kill the parakeet, and the dog didn't kill the cat?"

"All me," he said. He wasn't denying it. Something would have to change.

"What about Timothy?"

"I don't think he's in any danger."

My heart began to race. I was in danger, when he scratched at my bedroom door, when he stared at me while I watched cartoons. He'd growl if I forgot he was there.

"You're sure?" I could picture him nodding. My mother couldn't see the difference between his grins. "All right."

"He's my son, too."

I heard the rustle of their clothes as they embraced, my mother's sigh. Looking back, I wonder if she was too worn out to insist. How could she think it was all right? I wanted to run into their bedroom and grab onto her leg, but all I could have said was 'No daddy dog.'

One day there was a knock at the door. This wasn't unusual—deliveries, surveys, neighbors. The grin always got him through short visits. People assumed he was a good listener.

This time it was the Chins, the couple who lived in the next house. My father opened the door and said nothing. I stood a few feet behind him. It was like watching a dog stand on its hindlegs.

"Mind if we come in?" Ms. Chin asked.

My father stepped aside, closed the door behind them. I preferred this to being alone with him. He had to pretend to be a man when there were other adults around.

Mr. Chin walked past us into the kitchen. He didn't take his boots off, which normally would have bothered my father. "This is a nice house," he said, touching the wall, a doorknob, a painting. He looked back at me. "Do you like living here, Timmy?"

"Don't you mind all the trash bags on the curb?" Ms. Chin said.

I nodded, yes to both. I'd never really noticed the trash bags. I had other problems. But I couldn't just say 'No daddy dog.' They wouldn't have thought anything of it. Nor did I want to start everyone talking. It was good to have other adults over, but I didn't know what my father would do if grinning stopped working.

"None of the other houses have piles of trash in front," Mr. Chin said. "Someone takes it away for them."

"Does it get stinky, Timmy?"

"I could smell it from the porch."

I backed partway up the stairs. I was close to crying. I don't think they cared much if I cried, but it wasn't their goal.

"So," Ms. Chin said, turning to my father, "there are some houses for sale in the neighborhood."

He said nothing.

Ms. Chin looked to Mr. Chin. "At good prices," he said. "And bigger than this one." He waited a few seconds, and then added, "Regular trash collection." He looked back at Ms. Chin and shrugged. They knew they weren't being nice. The only one who didn't seem to get it was my father.

Mr. and Ms. Chin each took a step closer, and I took another step up the stairs.

"You don't have to go," Ms. Chin said. "We just want to talk."

Neither of them realized that my father's grin hadn't changed since he'd opened the door. It was when Mr. Chin put his hand on my father's shoulder that he noticed—my father could stand on two legs, but he couldn't change the way he moved, the way his whole body tensed at Mr. Chin's touch.

"Heh," Mr. Chin said. He watched me go up another step. I wished he would stop touching my father. I could tell that he wanted to, too, and that he wasn't going to. His boots had tracked dirt all the way into the kitchen, and he always seemed like he might spit. Pulling back his hand now was unimaginable. It was like it was stuck on my father's shoulder.

My father began to growl. I ran up to the top step, and Ms. Chin started to reach inside her jacket.

"We'll discuss it."

At first no one realized it was my father who had spoken. His mouth hadn't really moved. I hadn't thought he could speak when he was like this, and the Chins looked as surprised as I was. No one knew what would happen next.

"All right," Mr. Chin said, patting him on the back, squeezing his arm. "Good." Ms. Chin had already opened the door. My father stood facing them as they left, grinning.

That night my parents shouted at each other again. I sat on my dresser, listening through vent, waiting for them to hug, but they kept on shouting. I got down and started to pack my little monkey suitcase. If he ripped out her throat, I'd have no choice but to leave.

Suddenly the shouting stopped. They weren't talking. A minute or two went by, but their door didn't open. Maybe he'd been so quick she hadn't had the chance to scream. I zipped up my suitcase and climbed onto my dresser one last time.

I wouldn't have heard it at all had I not been listening—panting, like our real dog used to do when it was hot. It wasn't reason enough to leave. Instead, I got in my bed and, even though it was a few hours before my bedtime, lay there until I fell asleep.

After that the trash bags stopped piling up in front of our house, and the Chins never came back. I think they moved.

A few months later, my mother's belly began to swell. Even then I knew what it meant—a brother, a sister, maybe two or three. She was also walking around on all fours now. She liked to lie where the sun fell on the couch and lick her wrists. She'd hiss at me if I sat in her spot, or hugged her too suddenly, or didn't eat my meat. She was clearly going to give birth to a litter.

What followed was a time of dread. The two of them went on all fours more often than not, each grinning at nothing in particular. My mother didn't bother to push her hair back from her eyes. Soon I would be even more alone, without instincts, one against a pack. Soon I would be prey. I kept my little monkey suitcase packed.

One Sunday morning I was eating breakfast and looking at the comics. By now it was up to me to bring in the newspaper, among other things. My mother was in her spot on the couch, and my father was nosing under my arm, trying to get at my cereal. "No daddy dog," I said, but I knew it was no use.

The day I had to compete for food was the day I'd starve.

I blocked his face with my elbow, and he growled. I'd never resisted him before. We both knew how easily he could tear out my throat, but what choice did I have?

He nosed in again, and I tried to stop him with my hand, and he bit me. Nipped might be more precise. I wasn't bleeding, but that didn't matter—if I did nothing, then nothing was mine.

I looked at the toothmarks on my hand. How had man ever overcome beast? I was beginning to despair when it came to me—a memory from my recent year or two of awareness.

My grandmother on my father's side had a big dog, a mastiff. It was good-natured, better than either of my parents, but sometimes it got excited, especially during meals. My grandmother was strict. We've grown very close over the years.

I took the Sunday paper—the whole thing—rolled it into a tube and smacked my father on the ear. My mother raised her head to watch.

He growled, and I hit him again, and again, and again until he began to whimper. I had to stop myself—I hadn't felt so happy in months. Just holding up the paper brought his face to the floor. I could have chased him out of the house.

It's been a few years since that day. My parents still roam the house on all fours, but I don't feel unsafe anymore. I keep magazines in every room. I trained all of my brothers and sisters—quadruplets—to walk before they were one, not that any of them are big enough to scare me.

Eventually I realized that none of it was ever really that scary. Or, rather, it was no scarier than if my father had been acting like a man the whole time. Two, four, three, one—if he ever decides to rip out my throat, I won't be able to stop him no matter how many legs he's standing on.

Josh Taylor was born in Baltimore and now lives in France. His short stories have appeared in *Electric Spec*, *Metaphorosis*, and *The Penn Review*. Website: https://joshbtaylor.home.blog/

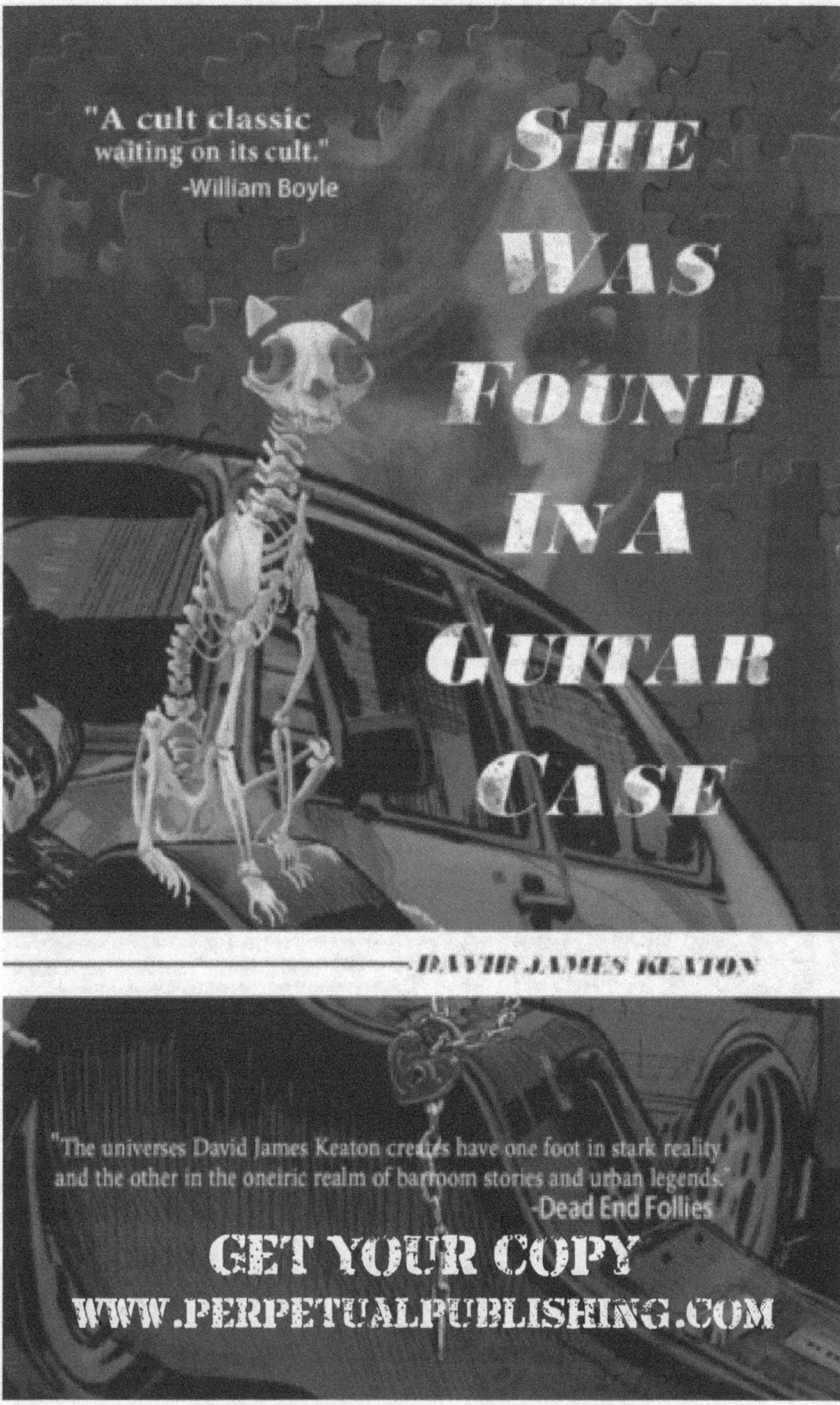
"A cult classic
waiting on its cult."
-William Boyle
SHE WAS FOUND IN A GUITAR CASE
DAVID JAMES KEATON
"The universes David James Keaton creates have one foot in stark reality
and the other in the oneiric realm of barroom stories and urban legends."
-Dead End Follies
GET YOUR COPY
WWW.PERPETUALPUBLISHING.COM

TRAVELERS
J.F. TUCKER

TOMAS AWOKE WITH a start and glanced at his watch. 5 p.m. Had he really slept that long? His head hurt and his muscles ached as he sat up and stretched. He felt like he'd just been in a train wreck. His foot brushed against a mound of dirty clothes when he swung his legs over the edge of the bed. He kicked them aside in disgust and headed straight for the medicine cabinet. He needed aspirin, and quick. He shook the bottle and breathed a sigh of relief when he heard at least one or two pills rattling around inside it. He quickly pried off the lid with his thumb and popped one into his mouth, swallowing it without water. *That should do it,* he thought as he gazed at himself in the mirror. With his pasty white skin and bloodshot eyes, he thought that he looked like death warmed over. He bent over the sink, splashed cold water on his face, and went back to his room. He stopped in front of his closet. He ran his hands through his hair and stared at a nearly empty row of hangers. He reached for a black, short-sleeved, collared shirt with white stripes and picked up a pair of jeans off the floor. He raised the latter to his nose and took a sniff. *Good enough,* he thought and put them on.

He stumbled into the tiny kitchen, which was also a mess. Dirty dishes were piled high in the sink and cartons of Chinese food, pizza boxes, and other miscellaneous take-out containers were strewn along the countertop. He lifted the corner of one of the boxes, and roaches scattered everywhere. *Gotta get someone in here to clean this shit up.* He opened a few cabinets and the refrigerator door. Empty. He cursed and slammed them shut, one by one. He closed his eyes and counted to ten. It didn't help.

"Fuck it," he said and eyed the front door. He swept up his car keys and wallet off the folding table which had become both a desk and dining area. On the way out, he kicked the trash can for good measure.

A cold gust of wind greeted him as he stepped outside the front door of his apartment. He shivered and looked up at the gray, gloomy sky. The neighborhood was eerily quiet and deserted. He looked to his right and saw that a dense curtain of fog was slowly beginning to envelop his apartment complex. He quickened his pace. After hopping into his car, he locked the doors and peeled out of his designated parking space.

He had no idea where he wanted to go or why. *Just drive,* he thought as he sped through rows of empty streets and shuttered businesses. When he got to the last stop sign in town, he spotted a young woman in her twenties standing by the side of the road with her thumb out. Although he knew better than to pick up hitchhikers, he thought that she looked harmless enough. He pulled over.

"Where you headed?" Tomas asked as he lowered the passenger window and leaned over.

The girl was wearing a white T-shirt and shorts and had wavy, brown hair and hazel-colored eyes. She bent down to meet his gaze and leaned her arms against the window frame. "Anywhere but here. Can you give me a lift?"

"Sure. Hop in," he replied as he unlocked the car door. "My name's Tomas. What's yours?"

"Julia," she said, sliding in with an outstretched hand. As he took it, it suddenly occurred to him that the sensation of her hand in his felt oddly familiar.

"Have we met before?" Tomas asked. Julia smiled and looked away as she placed her purse at her feet. *I guess that means no.*

They sat in companionable silence for the next few minutes as the windy two-lane road stretched out before them. The clouds overhead were dark and murky. Tomas wondered if it was going to rain.

Just then, two cars, one red and one black, zipped past him. The red car had a license plate which read *CATCHME*. He snorted in amusement and glanced at Julia, who had a visibly strained look on her face. She was clenching her fists as she watched the cars pull away and disappear into the mist.

Tomas tried to think of something to say to put Julia's mind at ease. "It's probably just a bunch of teenagers out for cheap thrills. Don't worry. I'll keep my eye out for them." He knocked on the top of his dashboard, adding, "I'm a very safe driver. No accidents or tickets. Ever. We'll be fine. Promise."

Julia glanced at him and seemed to relax somewhat. "I trust you."

At that moment, light rain began to fall onto the windshield. Tomas turned on the wipers and defroster. He was about to switch on the lights for better visibility when a large semitruck came barreling around a blind curve and into his lane. He laid on his horn in anger and flipped off the middle-aged truck driver, who was wearing a black-and-red plaid shirt and white baseball cap. He cursed loudly and jerked his car to the shoulder of the road, barely avoiding an accident. He hit the brakes hard and brought the car to an abrupt stop, throwing them both forward in their seats.

Meanwhile, the other driver rolled down his window as he drove by and yelled, "Fuck you, too, asshole."

Tomas scowled as he slammed the palm of his hand against the steering wheel and watched the semi fade from sight in his rearview mirror. He took a long, slow breath to calm his nerves then turned to Julia, who was white as a sheet, and asked, "Are you okay?"

"I'm fine." Julia looked shaken, but none the worse for wear. "How about you?"

Tomas sighed. "Have you ever had one of those days when you wish you'd never gotten out of bed?"

"That bad, eh?"

"So far, meeting you has been the only bright spot in what's been a totally crappy day."

"Have you heard the saying 'Misery loves company'?" Tomas nodded. Julia continued, "Then I guess we were destined to meet."

"What's your story?" Tomas asked, eyebrows raised.

Julia pursed her lips and shook her head. "It's complicated. You sure you want to hear it?"

Tomas glanced at the digital clock on the dashboard and said, "I've got nothing but time. At the rate we're going, we won't hit the next town for at least another half hour." Truth be told, he was in dire need of a distraction from their near miss and thought that listening to Julia's troubles would take his mind off things. Still, he didn't want to make her feel like he was putting her on the spot or trying to stick his nose into her business, and so he said, "It's totally up to you. We could just . . . "

Before he could finish his sentence, Julia replied, "Where would you like me to start?"

Tomas shrugged. "Wherever you want to," he said, then paused. "How about telling me how you ended up where I found you."

Julia nodded. "I moved here for my boyfriend. He got a teaching job at the local high school in town after we graduated from college."

"I see," Tomas replied. *A boyfriend, huh? I should've known. The good news is she likes teachers. I may have a shot.*

"We rented a one-bedroom apartment in the Whispering Palms Villas just off State Street."

"You did? I've got a place there, too." *Maybe that's why she seems so familiar. I must have seen her around the complex.*

Julia looked like she was unsure of what to say next. Finally, she said, "We had things all planned out, you know. We came here thinking we could start digging our way out of all the school debt we'd accumulated and build up a little nest egg before we got married. Neither of us was making much, but we got by. We had each other. That was the important thing."

"Sounds like you guys were a match made in heaven."

Julia shook her head. "It didn't start out that way. I was kind of seeing someone else the first time he asked me out, and so I said no. And then I saw him again a few weeks later. By that time, I'd broken things off with the other guy I'd been dating and so I invited him out for a cup of coffee."

"I assume he said yes."

Julia snorted. "No. Not at all. He turned me down flat."

Tomas smiled. "Good on him. I probably would've done the same thing."

"Luckily for me, he eventually came around and decided to take a chance on me. After that, we never looked back. At first, some of my closest friends and even my mom was concerned that we were getting too serious, too fast. I told them that I knew what I was doing and not to worry."

"So, what happened?" Tomas asked. *If everything between her and her boyfriend was as perfect as she's making it sound, what was she doing standing alone by the road trying to hitch her way out of town?*

Julia's lip quivered as she rested her head in her hand and stared out the window. And then a single tear ran down her cheek. She wiped it away and said, "He doesn't remember who I am. There was an accident and . . ."

Tomas reached out and touched Julia's hand. "It's okay. You don't have to tell me anything you don't want to." She turned to him with a faint smile. He added, "We'd better get back on the road. I have a feeling that the weather's going to get a lot worse tonight before it gets better."

As the car's lights illuminated the surrounding area, Tomas looked to his left and then glanced into the rearview mirror to make sure there was no oncoming traffic before he started to merge out onto the road. He hit the brakes and nearly jumped out of his seat the moment he caught sight of the same plaid-shirted truck driver who had just run him off the road standing behind his car. He quickly swung around. Nothing there but blackness and weeds. *I must be seeing things*. Still, he felt more than a little disconcerted.

He turned back around, took a deep breath, and slowly reentered the road. In the ensuing silence, he took the time to gather his thoughts. Everything about this day seemed wrong. From the moment he'd opened his eyes until their barely avoided disaster just now, he'd felt like he'd been cast adrift in a world which didn't make sense. The only exception was the beautiful and troubled stranger sitting next to him.

The stretch of road Tomas and Julia were on began to ascend into a mountainous area with enormous trees and steep embankments. For a second or two, he pictured his car veering off the road as they plummeted to their fiery death. *Where did* that *come from?* He batted the thought away, blaming it on residual nerves.

Minutes passed. Tomas sensed a growing unease in Julia. He could see it in her face and hear it in her breathing as she began to rock back and forth in her seat. *What's up with her?* he thought as he debated whether to reengage her in conversation. But just when he'd screwed up the nerve to open his mouth and speak, the sound of screeching tires and roaring engines coming up from behind made him pause and glance into his rearview mirror. From what he could see, it looked like there were two cars driving nearly parallel to each other at breakneck speed. Absent a miracle, he was sure that the car in his lane was going to rear-end him. He looked to the right to see if he could pull off the road again to avoid a collision but, to his dismay, there was no shoulder this time. What other, if any, options did he have? Knowing that time was running short, he gripped the steering wheel and stepped on the gas.

Tomas looked again into the mirror. The car directly behind his was moving over into the opposite lane of traffic. He said a prayer of thanks as he watched them pass. But as they began to disappear into the night, he caught sight of the license plate of the car that had been in his lane and froze. *CATCHME. That can't be right,* he thought as he struggled to convince himself that he wasn't losing his mind. In the meantime, he spotted a lookout point and immediately pulled over.

Tomas felt Julia's hand on his arm as soon as he turned off the engine. She reached over and touched his cheek with the back of her hand and said, "It's okay, Tomas. I'm here." He kissed her and pulled her close. She didn't resist. In fact, she seemed to welcome his advances with open arms. Several minutes passed before he finally broke their embrace and restarted the car. He stole glances in Julia's direction while working through the jumble of thoughts and feelings running through his mind and heart. Crazy as it seemed, he loved her with every fiber of his being, of that he had absolutely no doubt. And even though she hadn't said it outright, the way she'd kissed and held him made it obvious she felt the same way about him, too. *But what about her boyfriend?* The thought of that nameless and faceless person filled him with jealousy and guilt.

After a long silence, Tomas finally spoke up. "I'm sorry. I don't know what came over me . . . I hope this doesn't screw things up between you and your boyfriend."

"Don't worry about it," Julia replied matter-of-factly. "I was a perfectly willing participant. You have nothing to apologize for."

After careful consideration, Tomas said, "I like you. I like you a lot. I felt a real connection to you from the first minute I saw you."

"I felt it, too," Julia said as she placed her hand over his.

"So, where do we go from here?" Tomas asked. He knew he couldn't let Julia go. He was all in. *Whatever it takes, baby. Just say the word.*

As if she had read his thoughts, Julia replied, "I promised myself a long time ago that I'd do everything within my power to make my relationship with my boyfriend work. I mean to keep that promise. I owe him that."

Tomas nodded and said no more. *Time to move on, buddy. And don't even think about trying to argue with her.*

It was raining harder now. It was difficult to see, even with the windshield wipers at their highest setting. He let his foot off the gas and watched as the speedometer needle dropped from twenty-five mph to twenty to fifteen to ten . . .

And then, out of nowhere, Julia shouted, "Stop the car. Stop it NOW!"

Tomas glanced at her and then looked forward. He blinked again and again. *What the fuck?* his mind screamed as he tried to wrap his brain around the notion that the man in the red-and-black plaid shirt and white baseball cap was standing in the middle of the road. He jammed on the brakes, veered to the left, and prayed that no oncoming cars were nearby. *We're too close,* he thought and braced himself for impact. But when his vehicle finally came to a complete stop, the man was again nowhere to be seen.

With his heart thundering in his ears, Tomas looked at Julia and asked, "You saw him, right?"

"I have to go now," Julia replied and started to open the door. "This is where I get off."

Tomas grabbed her arm and said, "What do you mean? You can't leave now. We're out in the middle of nowhere and . . . and it's pouring outside. You're going to get drenched."

"Let me go." Julia had now become inconsolable. She yanked her arm away and picked up her purse as she bolted out of the car.

For a moment or two, Tomas was too stunned to move or speak. *What do I do now?* He raked his hands through his hair and tried to think. He looked down and saw Julia's cell phone lying on the floorboard where her feet had been. He picked it up and accidentally pressed the Home button. The lock screen appeared. What he saw shook him to his core. It was a picture of Julia . . . and him.

In an instant, it all came flooding back to him: two cars speeding past his in the pouring rain, the red car with the license plate *CATCHME* swerving out of control on the slippery, wet road; and the semitruck veering into his lane and hitting his car head-on. Worst of all, Julia's screams. *Oh God!*

Tomas got out of the car and shouted Julia's name over and over again until his voice was hoarse. "Where are you? I remember now. Please come back." He dropped to his knees and buried his face in his hands. He started to cry.

Suddenly, the rain stopped and the relentless wind ceased to blow. All was still, save for the sound of a wolf howling in the distance. It was then that Tomas felt the gentle pressure of Julia's hands on his shoulders. He turned and looked up at her.

"Why didn't you tell me?" Tomas's tone was neither accusatory nor angry.

"Would you have believed me if I did?"

Tomas paused, then asked, "So are we . . ."

Julia nodded and knelt down beside him. "It happened so fast. There was nothing you could've done to avoid it."

"Do you know where we are? It doesn't feel like heaven or hell."

Julia sighed. "I think we're somewhere in between. I saw a light right after it happened and heard a voice calling out to me. I started to walk toward it and then realized you weren't with me. I looked around and saw you walking away. You seemed so lost, and so when the voice beckoned me again to the light, I begged for more time. I couldn't move on, not without you."

Grabbing hold of both her arms, Tomas asked, "How many times have you had to live through this nightmare?"

"It doesn't matter," Julia replied and wept. "You would've done the same thing for me."

Tomas hung his head in shame. "I'm so sorry, baby . . . for everything."

"It's okay. We're going to be all right now. We're together. That's all that matters."

Tomas nodded and buried his face in Julia's shoulder. Moments later, he began to feel something warm and bright envelop them both. He looked up and gazed in wonder at the sight unfolding before his eyes.

Julia smiled and rose to her feet. She looked toward the light and held her hand out to Tomas. "It's time. Are you ready?"

Tomas nodded as he stood up and placed his hand in hers. And so they went, hand in hand, into eternity.

J.F. Tucker graduated from the University of California, Berkeley, and Notre Dame Law School. She was a Senate Fellow with the California Legislature and is a classically trained singer. Her debut novel, *Revelations*, was published in 2017.

AVAILABLE NOV 30, 2021
LOST CONTACT
EDITED BY MAX BOOTH III & LORI MICHELLE
WWW.PERPETUALPUBLISHING.COM

HOLE
SAM BARROWS

JACKSON FIRST NOTICED something wrong halfway through mowing his yard. His mower dipped beneath him: just a little dip, easily corrected, but then he took a step and felt the ground shift beneath his feet.

He shoved the puttering mower into the corner, killed the engine, and walked back to the center of his yard. As he approached, he tested the ground with his foot, and groaned when he felt a little give. Of course. Gophers or some shit. He just *knew* whatever this was had to be covered somewhere in the gargantuan homeowners association agreement he'd signed. It would be yet another problem for him to solve.

He didn't even want the damn lawn.

This gopher hole was just another landmine Missy had left him. They had both signed the HOA paperwork, but Missy had been the one dead-set on the suburbs, and Missy had been the one who squealed in delight during their one, all-too-brief tour. So he was comfortable blaming her. And of course Missy wasn't here to defend herself, which made it even easier. He wondered if she had dumped the ski instructor yet, if something younger and yummier had come along, and decided he didn't really want to know.

The homeowners association had seemed so harmless. They were a bunch of old fogies, looking like librarians or maybe history teachers, tweedy and as dry as scarecrows. They'd peered at him over their little glasses, *evaluating*. Would Joshua and Missy Jackson add to the *tone* of the neighborhood? Would they disrupt the bucolic harmony cultivated on Mulberry Street? Could they be trusted not to bring in barking dogs or squealing children? They could, as it happened. Kids weren't on the horizon, and Joshua was allergic to just about everything with fur. There were other requirements—home care, proper attention to one's lawn, respectful parking—but Jackson had waved those aside. Perhaps too quickly. He had never had a real lawn before, and the amount of labor it took to keep it "presentable" was quickly becoming an annoyance.

Missy had never given any outward sign that anything was wrong. Of course, she wouldn't, would she? She was an actress, and a good one. Better than Jackson had expected, if she'd been able to conceal not *one*, not *two*, but *three* concurrent affairs not only from her husband, but from each other as well. When the penny had dropped, she'd at least had the good grace to look abashed. She'd cried a little, but Jackson couldn't tell her fake tears from real ones, and he didn't care. She didn't want the house and there weren't any kids or pets to split, so *au revoir*, Missy. Have fun in Aspen or wherever.

So here was Jackson, with a house just a bit too big for him and a backyard he was rapidly growing to hate. He knelt down and rested a hand on the turf. It was springy here, loose, and as he watched, a few crumbles of earth shifted. He squinted. There was a damn hole about the size of a damn golf ball right in the damn middle of his damn lawn.

He mostly stayed off the lawn during the week. He was busy at work, and it was still a little too cold to grill out there. Spring had sprung, but winter was taking its time slinking out the back door. So it was a week before he got out there again, and during that time he thought of the hole maybe once. It was subsumed under the tidal wave of minor domestic bullshit swamping any first-time homeowner, especially in the suburbs, and *especially* especially with a HOA who crawled up his ass for fun.

When Jackson returned to his lawn, it wasn't to mow or address the hole, but just to stretch his legs. He had been working from home that day, enjoying the peace and quiet while he hammered out a personal injury settlement, and he needed some fresh air. In fact, he had completely forgotten about the hole until he nearly tripped in it. His foot slipped, he waved his arms like a cartoon character for a moment, but somehow he kept his balance. The hole was the size of a baseball now, and the turf around it noticeably canted inward. "Fuck," he muttered. This wasn't going to go away on its own.

That night he ordered ultrasonic toadstools. They looked like toadstools, anyways, so that was what he was calling them. You planted them in your yard and they were supposed to send out little vibrations to get rid of gophers and moles and things. He'd plant them right up against the fence and that would be that. In the meantime, he'd fill in the hole with some sod or something.

So the next day—a beautiful Saturday when he really *should* have been enjoying a beer on his couch—he took his Beamer out to the Home Depot and stood around the gardening section looking clueless until a young man in an orange vest took pity on him.

"Can I help you, sir?" the boy asked, all chipper enthusiasm.

Jackson looked him up and down and, conscious of how ridiculous he sounded, said "I want to buy some dirt."

To his credit, the boy didn't laugh. He just looked at Jackson in polite incomprehension. "Dirt, sir?"

"Yeah," said Jackson. "Dirt. Earth, whatever. It's for a hole in my backyard."

"Oh. You want topsoil," the boy said, and gave him a relieved smile. "That's right over here. I can get you a cart."

Dirt turned out to be more expensive than Jackson would have believed. He bought two bags, just to be sure, and an attendant carried them out to his car. He hadn't thought about putting two bags of dirt in the Beamer's trunk, and he grimaced at the thought of it grinding into the carpeting. "Careful with that stuff," he said as the attendant manhandled the bags into the trunk. The guy gave him a weird look. *Hah, yeah, don't hurt my precious dirt,* Jackson thought. *HOA will kill me if I put damaged dirt in the yard.* The thought made him snort.

Back at home, he changed into an old T-shirt and dug his work gloves out of the garage before unloading the car. In addition to being expensive, dirt was heavy as hell, but eventually he got both bags back to the yard. He slit the top of one with a pair of shears and tipped the bag over. It slid downward; the hole was about the size of a grapefruit now, sitting at the bottom of a depression.

Jackson watched carefully as the dirt trickled out. Eyeballing the hole, he figured half a bag might be enough—he'd always been a thorough planner, though, and better safe than sorry. The first three-quarters of a bag, though, just disappeared into the darkness. He shook the last few clods out of the bag and tossed it aside, then looked down into the hole.

Nothing. It was pitch black in there. He pulled out his phone and turned on the flashlight, then crouched over the hole. If it was a gopher tunnel, it was the weirdest one he'd ever seen. It simply went down, straight down, past the limits of his light. The walls were bare and smooth. There was no sign of any of the dirt he'd poured into it. He grunted and made to stood. Just before he did, a breeze puffed across his face—brief, but much warmer than the early-spring weather. For a second, he thought it came out of the hole, then dismissed the idea as ridiculous. He slit the top of the second bag and began to pour.

The hole swallowed this offering, too. He held the bag up by its last corner as the last few clumps tumbled out, shook it to make sure it was empty, then let it drop. Once again, he squatted; once again, he produced his phone. Still nothing. The hole looked exactly the same as it had before he'd dumped the second bag.

What was this, anyways? Some kind of breach into the city sewer? He just *knew* he'd catch hell for it with the HOA, even if it wasn't his fault. The thought of driving back to Home Depot didn't appeal. He'd wasted enough time on the damn thing. He'd plant his gopher toadstools and then think of his next move.

It took them another week to arrive, during which time the hole expanded from baseball to volleyball sized. There was a definite pit around it, too, like an antlion's den. Nothing lived in holes like that, right? It was probably . . . water erosion or something. Something in the sewer had broken or collapsed and it just happened to be under Joshua Jackson's lawn. Because that was how things worked. As he was striding out to plant his toadstools, a voice called out from the other side of his stockade fence. "Hey, neighbor!"

The fence was low enough for a grown man to lean over the top, and Frasier Gill was doing so now. Jackson groaned inwardly. Gill wasn't a bad guy, though it was impossible not to note a resemblance to Ned Flanders from *The Simpsons*. *I swear to God if he ever calls me neighborino I'm gonna chuck something at him*, Jackson thought. Instead, he forced himself to smile back. "Hello, Frasier," he said.

"Doing some lawn care? I should follow your example. Winter really messed up the wife's herb garden," Gill said.

Come on, Frasier, Jackson thought. *It fucked up your wife's stupid plants. Just swear like a normal person. I don't have kids and yours are at school, so just talk like you aren't about to break out in "diddlies."*

"Yeah," he said. "Just trying to keep ahead of the HOA. You know how it is."

"Sure do!" Gill said with an enthusiastic nod. "Looks like you've got moles or something." He pointed at the hole. Jackson, who was starting to conclude that he didn't have moles at all, nodded.

"Probably. I got these sonic things to chase them off." He pointed at his purchases.

Gill smacked the fence with one hand. "Wow! You're ahead of the curve, man! I was just gonna suggest some mothballs! My mother always said that got rid of them real fast."

Jackson nodded and grunted, about the extent of answer he felt that statement deserved.

"Well," said Gill, "Good luck. If they pop up in my yard I'll let you know."

"Thanks, Frasier," said Jackson. Before the man could rope him into another conversation, he went inside. His evening had been set aside for reviewing a deposition in a slip-and-fall case, and while he had been putting it off for as long as possible, right now he was eager to start. As soon as he sat down at his desk, though, his focus evaporated. He found his thoughts returning again and again to the hole. *Fucking sewer. Fucking city. What do I pay my taxes for?*

That night he found himself dreaming. It was summertime, and he was hosting a barbecue in his backyard. He wore a huge KISS THE COOK apron and a chef's toque like the dad from some cartoon sitcom. Everyone was there, crowded around the modest yard: Frasier Gill, the other neighbors, the prune-faced old HOA board, even his current client and the judge from his last case. A couple of paralegals from the office were handing out buns and cups of beer. The hole was still there in the middle of his yard—in fact, it was larger, about as big around as a manhole cover. Nobody commented on it. They all just navigated around it without looking down. Jackson was standing by the grill flipping burgers when a high-pitched voice made him start. "Joshua!" it said. "Great to see you! Thanks soooooo much for inviting us!"

It was Missy. She was wearing a little sundress, the kind she always used to break out as soon as it got hot enough. Missy threw her arms out for a hug. "Dah-ling!" she said. "It's been an age! Come here!" She began to cross the yard, and before Jackson could say anything, she had stepped into the little bowl-shaped depression around the hole. Her expression changed from delight to horror in an instant, and she began to tumble forward. Her legs disappeared into the hole and her upper body thumped down hard on the lip. Her fingers dug into the turf, pulling up little curls of grass. "You asshole!" she shrieked. "I coulda been killed! I'm gonna sue you! Sue you! Sue you!"

The rest of the crowd was chanting now, too: "Sue! Sue! Sue!" Jackson raised his arms to protest, waving them protectively in front of his face, but his cries were drowned out by the crowd. "Sue! Sue! Sue!" Mr. Kerchick of the HOA stood in front of him, an imposing figure despite his advanced age, now somehow wearing a judge's robes and holding a gavel. "Mr. Jackson, I find you guilty of violating your agreement!" he said in a voice like thunder. Jackson tried to protest, but the dark iris of the hole opened up before him and the words dried up in his mouth.

He awoke in a cold sweat. The digital clock by the bed showed 6:09AM, but he knew he would not be going back to sleep. He lay there until his heart rate slowed, then got up for a glass of water.

As he had expected, the sonic toadstools didn't work. If anything, they made things worse. In the previous week, the hole had gone from baseball to volleyball. Now, a day later, it was the size of a beach ball. As he watched, a bit of dirt crumbled from the lip and fell in. He shook his head, but the dream was still replaying in his mind and he didn't want to get any closer to the hole than he had to. *Tonight*, he told himself, *I'll call the city*.

Work was agonizing. He spent the whole day distracted, reading the same few lines over and over. A new possibility had occurred to him: in addition to being in trouble with the HOA, he would be in hot shit with the city. Somehow, in the course of attempting to stay on the good side of his neighbors, he had broken or damaged something underground. He'd have to pay for whatever it was. He could see his retainer disappearing, and whatever extra he managed to squeeze out of his latest settlement. The unfairness of it galled him.

He cut out early and dialed the number from the city website. The phone rang twice, then a bored-sounding voice said, "Department of Power and Water, can you state the nature of your problem?"

Jackson tried to lay it out as simply as he could. Yes, a hole. Yes, his backyard. A couple of weeks ago. No, no wetness around it, no strange smells. He gave his address and waited while the clerk punched it in.

"Uh, sir, we're not showing that we have any pipes or lines running beneath your backyard."

The massive payment, the one he had already deducted from his mental bank account, vanished like a weight from his shoulders. In its place, unease crept in.

"Nothing?" he asked. "No tunnels or whatever?"

"Uh, no sir," said the voice. "We've got nothing back there. It might just be gophers."

"Gophers," said Jackson. "Okay. Maybe. Thank you. You've been very helpful." He hung up and then sat there staring at the wall.

Okay. No tunnel. No moles. So . . . what?

He didn't have an answer and didn't like thinking about it. Instead, he grabbed a beer, turned on the TV, and ordered pizza. What the hell, right?

The letter arrived the next day.

His address was listed out in cursive script. **Joshua Jackson, 18 Mulberry St.** There was no return address, but that was OKAY, because there was no postmark either. No mailman had brought this particular missive to his doorstep. Why would they have to? The HOA board all lived on this street.

He knew what it was going to say before he opened it, but he still sat down at the kitchen table for form's sake. The letter inside was a single tri-folded piece of printer paper—no header, no signature, just neat lines of text.

Dear Neighbor,

We have enjoyed having you living with us in our community here. However, we have recently become aware of an issue with your lawn. The hole is, unsightly and detracts from your neighbors enjoyment of their own backyards—and, should you have guests over, it poses a serious hazard.

We pride ourselves on keeping a safe and friendly community. Everyone living on Mulberry Street is part of one big family, and so our concern should be taken as it was intended: a well-intentioned hint to tackle a small problem before it becomes a big one!

We trust that you will take care of this issue posthaste. Mulberry Street is a great place to live, and we know you share our commitment to keeping it beautiful.

Yours sincerely,
The Mulberry Street Homeowners Association

Jackson sat for five minutes with the letter gripped tightly in his hands. At the end of that time he very slowly and carefully ripped it down the middle into two equal-sized pieces. These he dropped in the recycling bin. He then returned to the kitchen table and sat, staring at the wall, for nearly half an hour. Finally, he got up and fished around in his file cabinet until he found the HOA paperwork he had signed when closing on the house.

It made for interesting reading. It took him two hours to find what he was looking for, and another forty minutes of patient cross-checking to make sure he hadn't missed anything. He had work to do, but it would keep. He carefully noted down the page numbers in question, filed the paperwork away, and then pulled out his phone.

The contractors arrived early Saturday. The man Jackson had spoken to took one look at the backyard and scratched his head. "Uh, you want us to tear down the old fence?" he said. Jackson shrugged.

"If you have to. Can you just build on top of it? I want it to be at least ten feet high."

"Ten feet?" The guy stared at Jackson's face, as if looking for a hint he was kidding. "Are you sure, man? Won't your neighbors complain?"

Jackson held his gaze steady. "Fuck 'em," he said in a low, deadpan voice. The contractor chuckled, but he looked away all the same. Jackson's stare was unsettling.

"Yeah, we can put it up, sure," he said. "Take us a day or two."

Jackson waved him off. "Take as long as you want. Can you start today?"

"Nah, tomorrow. Gotta pull permits and stuff."

Jackson nodded. "Okay. Fair enough." He held out his hand to shake, and after a moment's hesitation, the contractor took it. As he walked back to his truck, the contractor looked over his shoulder. "You know, you got a nasty sinkhole back there. You want us to take a look at it?"

"No thanks," Jackson called after him. "I'm taking care of it."

That night he had a hard time getting to sleep. He kept thinking about the hole. He had gone out to check on it after dinner. By now it was at least as large as it had been in his dream. Finally, around midnight, he got up and snuck downstairs, feeling like a burglar in his own home. He slid the back door open and stepped out in his bare feet, shivering slightly at the cold. The hole was somewhere ahead of him, a patch of deeper black against the night. He pulled out his phone again and flicked on the flashlight. There it was. Larger than this afternoon? Hard to tell, but he thought so. He shuffled forward and knelt by its edge. It was perfectly round and perfectly smooth. It still descended into infinite blackness, but when he played the beam of his light over the walls, he thought he saw something new. Was there . . . something bulging out of the wall? Not like a rock or stick. It looked like a nub, like a parasite burrowed under the flesh of the wall. He reached down to touch it and froze with his hand a few inches away. He shook his head, as if awakening from a dream, and stood up quickly. One last look at the hole and he scurried inside.

The contractors were busy all the next day and the day after that, so Jackson worked at the office. He was barely functional; he drummed his fingers on his desk and got up to pace every twenty minutes. The thought of the wall going up around his yard had him as giddy as a kid on Christmas. He had asked the contractors to run it right up against the wall of his house, and had strenuously rejected their offers to put in a gate or window. "All around," he'd said. "Full coverage." They looked at him as if he was nuts, but for what he was paying them, they knew better than to question. He'd left them a cooler of beer on the back porch, and it was empty when he got home.

The fence was done when he got home, too. Ten feet of solid brown wood with that piney fresh-cut smell still clinging to it. Without any kind of adornment it looked sinister, like the wall of a prison. He especially liked the way his house seemed to jut out from it. It reminded him of pictures he'd seen of castle gatehouses. His home looked stronger now, fortified, if only by a couple of inches of wood. He approved. A man's home was his castle, right?

The second letter arrived that night.

Dear Neighbor, read Jackson, holding the letter in hands he didn't realize were trembling. *We have noticed your recent construction project. As you are no doubt aware, the homeowners covenant you signed strictly forbids such construction. We understand that you may be having some difficulties with your lawn, but this is not an acceptable solution. Please restore your lawn's old appearance before we must resort to legal action.*

"Nope," said Jackson to himself. "Nope, nope, nope." He chuckled quietly. The covenant he had signed—and read, carefully, with a lawyer's eye for detail—did *not* strictly forbid such construction. It forbade lots of things, and laid out mandates for lots more, but he had read the entire section on "fences, walls and barriers" five times. There were rules about material, rules about decor, rules about property lines and gate placement . . . but there was no restriction on height.

None at all.

"Sorry, HOA!" Jackson whispered in his empty kitchen. "You lose this one." He threw the new letter away, then went into his office and typed a response. He thought it was appropriately restrained and avoided unnecessary profanity. When he had finished, he sealed it in an envelope, wrote H.O.A. on the front in shaky block capitals, and laid it on the front table. The next day he'd drop it off at Mr. Kerchick's house. He had errands to run anyways.

Kerchick either wasn't home or, more likely, had been watching through the curtains and wouldn't come to the door for Jackson. Whistling, Jackson tucked the letter in the mail slot and headed back to his car. He heard the slot clink as he opened his car door and smiled to himself.

His next step was Home Depot. He had a short list, and it was easy to find what he was looking for. He loaded it all in his trunk and took quick inventory: one pair of work gloves, one heavy duty gardening shovel, three sets of 1000 watt work lights, three extension cords, and a 100 Grand Bar. He gnawed on the bar as he drove home, tossed the wrapper out the window, and turned on the radio. It was just some poppy crap, but he tapped his fingers on the the whole way home.

He briefly regretted the lack of a gate as he struggled to carry the heavy lights through the house. Once they were all set up, though, he took a moment to look around the backyard and felt vindicated. With the high walls and the lights, it felt more than ever like a prison yard, and that was good. That was what he was going for. Nothing in here was going to get out, and no nosy neighbors were going to see in. Now, he could work in peace and quiet.

Surveying the lawn, he was not surprised to see the hole was nearly two feet across now and sat at the bottom of a shallow bowl-shaped depression nearly the width of the yard. Subsidence, it was called. He remembered that from a slip-and-fall case a few years ago. Subsidence: the gradual sinking or caving in of a piece of land. Well, his backyard was subsiding for a reason, and he was going to figure out what it was.

The work was tough at first. The earth was still hard from winter, and his shovel barely bit into it. He was reduced to flicking chunks of earth free with the tip. His cotton work shirt was quickly soaked with sweat, but when he took it off he shivered in the spring breeze. At least disposing of the dirt was easy enough; he just tossed it in the hole. As before, it vanished without a sign, not even a delayed splash or thud as it hit the bottom. Maybe the hole was bottomless. "Don't be ridiculous," Jackson said out loud. "Nothing's bottomless."

He kept at it for three hours, until his hands were blistered and his arms were so sore he could barely raise the shovel. Then he planted the blade in the earth and raised his head. The walls towering over him on all sides made him feel as though he was at the bottom of the hole himself. What little of the sky he could see was orange-red, and the light from above was fading. He'd bought the work lights so he could dig after dark, but not tonight. He had made a good start.

Looking around, he was disappointed to see how little he'd actually cleared. Digging down, all he'd found was more dirt. But he knew he was on the right track. The hole wasn't bottomless and it wasn't infinite. It had limits, and he was going to reach them.

That was how he spent the next two weeks. He went to the office most days, but he never stayed later than five o'clock. He'd drive home, park, microwave a meal, and immediately set to digging. Sometimes he'd put in an hour or two and knock off for the night. Sometimes he'd quit, go grab a beer, then come back for a second shift in the dark. More and more often, he'd simply work through until he teetered on the brink of collapse. He was getting closer, he could feel it.

The hole was nearly six feet across at this point. The texture of its walls was very definitely not earth. It looked like stone or concrete, great curved slabs of it. The lines between them were so faint as to be practically invisible. Maybe it *was* just dirt, but Jackson didn't think so.

No, he didn't think so at all.

There were more nubs in the wall, too. They extruded from the wall in pairs about eighteen inches apart. To Jackson, they looked like little horns or hooks curving in towards each other. He still didn't dare touch them. They glistened and caught the light strangely—sometimes he thought he saw them move out of the corner of his eye. No matter how far down Jackson dug, he only found more dirt, but there was no denying the rapid pace of the hole's expansion since he'd begun. Maybe he was freeing it, he thought. Clearing off the imprisoning earth, helping it create itself. This idea had a kind of dream-logic appeal.

There had been no answering letter from the HOA. He figured they were consulting a lawyer and allowed himself a chuckle at the thought. Any lawyer would tell them what Jackson himself had figured out: his loophole was ironclad. They couldn't touch him—not with the HOA contract, anyways. He could dig all he wanted.

The dreams were becoming a bit of a problem, though. He still dreamed of his backyard as it looked now. He was shoved back into one corner, trapped against his fence. Strange figures shambled aimlessly around the yard, moaning in low and guttural voices. They were dressed in fine and fancy clothes, but dirty and unkempt, as though they had been buried in them. Worst of all were their heads: featureless, with the texture of dirt, like living chunks of earth who had torn themselves free to walk under the sun. They circled the hole in an endless, trudging procession, moaning and whimpering and swaying back and forth.

One night he awoke from such a dream to find himself standing in his backyard. At first, he was unsure if he was still dreaming. He had never sleepwalked before, and his bedroom was on the second floor. But the sudden blast of cool air in his face had woken him up, and he stood ramrod-straight for a moment. He was on the very lip of the pit. As he gathered his composure, a gust of hot air blew up out of it and into his face. It carried with it a dry, spicy smell, the smell of a desert, the smell of a mummy clawing its way free from its tomb. It lingered on his nostrils for a second and was gone, leaving only the wet-grass smell of spring.

Jackson hunched down and peered into the hole. The moon was bright tonight and directly overhead, giving him a reasonable amount of light to see by. The bulging protrusions on the side of the hole had grown further, and there was no mistaking them now. They looked delicate, but he supposed that was because they weren't finished growing yet.

They were rungs.

By the time the sun rose the next morning, Jackson had already finished his preparations. Today was the day, he could tell. He hadn't been able to get back to sleep the night before, but he wasn't tired. In fact, he was practically bursting with energy. He ate a big bowl of cereal, drank a tall glass of water, changed into fresh work clothes and headed out into his backyard. There was *so little* work left. He estimated a few hours, that was it. When he closed his eyes, he could feel his body thrumming with energy. He was on the verge of something, he knew it, some kind of breakthrough.

His shovel had barely broken the earth, however, when the doorbell rang. He almost cried in frustration. To be this close, and to be called away! He almost ignored it, but as he lowered the blade to the turf again, he heard a second ring and a faint hammering on the door. Jackson sighed, laid his shovel against his shoulder, and turned around.

One glance through the spyhole confirmed his suspicions. Mr. Kerchick was out there, holding a manila envelope in his hands. Behind him were the rest of the HOA board: Mr. Plotz, Mrs. Simpkin, Mrs. Dray, Mr. Barnard. And Frasier Gill, looking guilty and knotting his fingers together in front of him. Jackson's lips pulled back from his teeth in an animal grimace. He forced it into something resembling a smile and opened the door.

"Mr. Kerchick! And the rest of you. Good morning to you all. How can I help you?" he said, in his best "talking to juries" voice. Kerchick looked up at him with beady, querulous eyes.

"Is that a shovel, Jackson?" he asked. Jackson held out his shovel as though he had never seen it before.

"What, this? Oh, yes. I'm just doing some yard work. You know how it is. Busy, busy. Gotta keep up standards."

"Yes, well, that's why I've come to see you," Kerchick said. He held out the envelope. "This is an order from the city. That fence is in violation of building codes for this neighborhood and it has to come down."

Jackson made no move to take the letter. "Hm. Interesting. I think I'll decline, though, Kerchick. I need my fence."

"Decline?" Kerchick asked, scowling. "You can't *decline*, you ninny. Tear that thing down or I'm calling the police."

"Come on, Joshua," said Gill. Desperate pleading was written all over his face. "Just get rid of it. We aren't going to try to make you sell or anything, we just want the fence gone."

Kerchick brandished the envelope like a weapon. "Take it, Jackson," he snarled. "Take it and call your damn contractors. Or don't. Whatever Gill says, I'd love to see the back of you."

Jackson pondered this for a moment with a thoughtful expression on his face. Then he hefted the shovel and swung it as hard as he could into Kerchick's head.

The old man didn't even see it coming. There was a loud *clang* and an impact which reverberated up Jackson's arm. Kerchick staggered back for a moment, then collapsed bonelessly to the ground. His skull hit Jackson's porch step with a thick *crunch* and he sprawled at an odd angle. Jackson could see a thin ring of blood in the middle of the shovel, like a lipstick kiss. It oozed between the dirt granules already stuck to the blade. One of the old ladies screamed. Frasier Gill and the others staggered backwards, leaving Jackson and the prone Kerchick at the middle of a widening ring. One of the old man's arms was sticking out straight, still holding his letter.

Jackson didn't wait for the tension to break. He dropped the shovel with a clatter and darted inside. His movement broke Gill's paralysis, but he slammed the door and shot the bolts home a moment before the knob started to rattle. From outside, he could hear more screaming, and angry shouts, muffled by the door.

Moving on autopilot, he walked into his kitchen and pulled on the backpack sitting on the counter. He had hoped to have more time to pack, maybe to change clothes, but someone would certainly have called the police by now. In a nice neighborhood like this, they'd be here in no time. He had to trust that he'd thought of everything.

In his backyard, he paused at the edge of the pit. The rungs looked fully grown now, only a hint of wet shine on them to suggest they hadn't been there all along. They descended down as far as he could see. The sun was right overhead, and he could see quite a long way . . . but at the end of that long, long stretch of rungs, the hole vanished into darkness. He looked up one more time at the sun, felt the spring breeze on his face, and closed his eyes.

Then, carefully gripping the top rung, he lowered himself into the hole and began to climb.

Sam Barrows' writing has appeared in *Andromeda Spaceways* magazine. He lives with his wife, a cat, and a gigantic bunny rabbit in Boston Massachusetts, and when not writing, works as an attorney

THE
FOREST
LISA QUIGLEY

And now, an exclusive excerpt of *The Forest* by Lisa Quigley,available from Perpetual Motion Machine

Chapter One

Present

CHARLIE IS SLEEPING like the dead. I take his pulse to make sure he's still alive, that I haven't inadvertently killed him. Protecting Jonas is my top priority, but I would much rather do so without slaughtering the man who, up until two days ago, I deeply loved.

There is a sharp stab in my groin, wild emotion manifested as physical pain.

Of course, I still love him. That's not something that just goes away.

But he has betrayed me in a way I could have never anticipated, and that's a wound that won't heal easily. Probably not ever.

The dark, abysmal depression sucks at me. If I allow myself to submerge, I may never find my way back out.

I won't think about Charlie. There isn't time to be heart sick.

I have changed into brown corduroy pants, a grey thermal shirt, and a green and brown flannel shirt. Over that, I wear my warm green jacket. Neutral colors. Forest colors. I want to blend in. To be camouflaged. It is early fall, yes, but the forest is still green with only the faintest whispers of yellow. It's been unseasonably warm this month—a small grace for which, at this moment, I feel unbearably grateful—but it still gets chilly at night, and this time of year, the weather can be unpredictable. I am wearing waterproof hiking boots, and warm wool socks. Charlie's knife is tucked into my back pocket.

It's for food, I tell myself. In an emergency, I can kill a rabbit or squirrel. The thought makes me squeamish, but I will do what I need to be nourished. To stay alive for my son, I can do it. I could do anything for him.

I already am.

I go into the kitchen and chug a glass of water. "Better to carry water in your body than on it," Charlie told me once, when he was sharing his wilderness survival skills. Always a forest explorer and adventurer in my own right, I never really had to worry about danger in Edgewood's borders. I am grateful for his insights, now, and I hope they serve me well.

Next, I collect Jonas from his perch on my bedroom floor. He, too, is dressed in warm layers, and his body is soft and drooping. He is tired. My stomach churns. Adjusting to the lack of sleep in those early newborn days had been the most grueling part of early parenthood. Neither Charlie nor I had ever experienced anything like it. But with consistency (and, at times, pure desperation) we'd finally gotten him into a routine that allowed us all some blissful rest.

The amount he sleeps now is a blessing compared to those early days and since finding a schedule and routine that works, I've been so careful to adhere to it. But I don't have a choice. I am hoping he will sleep the night strapped to my chest, while I walk for as long and as far as I can tonight. I only have a very small window to get ahead and I must make it count.

Soon, they'll realize that I'm gone.

I strap Jonas into the baby carrier, his belly pressed up against my own. He settles his left cheek against my breast and I give him a pacifier. Already his eyelids are drooping.

Once I am wearing Jonas, I pull on a wool hat. Then I hoist the backpack over my shoulders. Even though I've only packed essentials, it's heavier than I would have liked. It will have to do.

Jonas' eyelashes, like downy feathers, rest on his cheek. I kiss the top of his head, which is protected by a warm cap.

"Let's go, baby boy," I whisper. "We're going on an adventure."

I was hoping the words would cheer me up, but they just make me feel worse. Resolve curdles and solidifies in my groin.

There is no changing my mind now.

I step onto the porch. It is already dark out, and the entrance to the wooded trail is about fifty feet away from our back door.

The trailhead seems to yawn, stretching open like a wide, black mouth.

My pulse quickens.

I rub the gentle curve of Jonas' spine instinctively.

I love the woods, but I have always held a healthy respect for the woods at night. The woods at night are not always a friendly place for humans.

I try not to think about what might be living in there, besides animals. What might be waiting for me just inside that inky blackness.

Stop it.

I blink and swallow.

These dark thoughts are not helping anyone. Least of all myself. My pulse throbs. I am afraid. There. I thought it, I've admitted it. Now it's time to let it go, to move past it.

It's time to enter the dark forest.

I reach for the large wooden walking stick we keep by the back door. *For support*, I tell myself. *To help with my burden.*

And behind that thought, another: *To beat off anything that wishes to do us harm.*

And just as I descend the final step, a figure emerges from behind the house, blocking my path.

"I had a feeling you might try to leave."

It's my mother.

Chapter Two

Before the Forest

MY BABY IS DEAD.

The thought vibrated against my skull, loud and immediate. I stabbed a piece of popcorn with my needle, focusing on the satisfying way it slid through to the other side. My hands shook.

My baby died while I was laughing.

I impaled another piece of popcorn, this time so violently I pricked my finger with the needle. A red pearl formed on my fingertip, and I lifted it to my mouth. Suck. Drew in a trembling breath.

These thoughts were terrible, and they were also lies.

Jonas was in the living room, strapped to my husband's chest in the canvas baby carrier. Relinquishing control, giving Charlie space to be a father—these were things I'd been working on. That it took so much focused effort was astonishing. Logically I knew the absurdity of the panic that surged in my chest when my son wasn't in my direct line of sight, or better, physically connected to me. *Knowing* didn't make my fear any less real. The intrusive thoughts were relentless. It was irrational to believe my baby wasn't safe. We were in Edgewood, after all.

Charlie's mother had been helping me work through it. She was the only one I was not ashamed to tell. She had been on the brink of death when they arrived in Edgewood. Stage four cancer in her breasts, her lymph nodes, her ovaries—the specific kind of horrific that most people only read about on the news, but which Charlie's mother—and, by proxy, her family—had to live through. Being from outside of Edgewood, she understood what was happening to me. *Postpartum anxiety*. She told me, though, I had to trust Charlie's love for our son, his instincts as a father, despite my worry. Charlie had to find his own way into fatherhood.

She was right, of course.

Or so I had believed.

I was making strands of popcorn garlands with my siblings in preparation for the fall festival. Lengths of our assembled garland looped over the ends of the table and a giant bowl of popcorn that Blossom just refreshed was at the table's center. This moment was nostalgic, familiar, yet I felt myself as incongruous within it. Everything was the same as it had been my whole life. I was the one who had changed.

The music that is my whole family surrounded me, but all I felt was the gaping absence where Jonas should be.

My skin itched. Did Charlie know to make sure Jonas' nose wasn't blocked by the carrier? A vein in my neck throbbed. Would Charlie place his hand on Jonas' back to ensure it still rose and fell? I wiped damp hands on my jeans. What if Charlie wasn't vigilant? I pictured us releasing Jonas from the carrier to discover that he was cold and blue and *it was too late*. My teeth vibrated. My hands returned to the table. I stabbed another piece of popcorn.

But it wasn't popcorn. Jonas' skin was blue and when I reached for him, I forgot the needle. My hand slipped and it punctured my dead baby's eyeball. It oozed clear, thick liquid.

I gasped and dropped the needle.

My stomach hitched; my chest tightened. My pulse throbbed against my neck and I squeezed my eyes shut but it was too late. The images were burned into my memory, real as though they'd actually happened.

My insides churned with shame. Where were these images coming from? Why did every single mundane thing I did lead to perpetual scenarios of impending doom?

My baby could be dead and I'd have done nothing to stop it.

The thought that I'd have the audacity to sit there and laugh with Arrow and Blossom, *to enjoy myself*, while my baby slipped away from this world was unbearable.

I stabbed a piece of popcorn so fiercely it split in two.

The light smack of something soft hitting me in the center of my forehead startled me. I breathed in deeply to absorb the depth of the aromas of cinnamon and pumpkin and yeast mingling in my mother's warm kitchen to ground myself in the comfort of home.

"What did that popcorn ever do to you?" It was Blossom. Beneath her mirthful teasing was something more serious: concern.

I blushed. "Nothing. Overeager."

The offending object that hit my forehead was now on the table in front of me: a particularly plump piece of popcorn. I picked it up. Arrow sat across from me, his fire-brown eyes watching me with a mixture of mockery and something else, something more intense that disquieted me.

Blossom, sitting next to me at the table, playfully jabbed a finger into my side.

"Earth to Faye." Her face was round, her cheeks pink—possibly from the warmth of the kitchen and definitely from youth, but also from the half glass of wine that Mom allowed her to have. She's turning twenty-one later this year; she's six years younger than me and it is always hard for me to believe that the plump face of this gorgeous young woman belongs to my baby sister. I could still hear the way my mother wailed when Blossom made her entrance into this world.

The abyss was ever near, drawing me closer with a magnetic roar that filled up my ears with buzzing. It was hungry for me, feeding on me from the inside out. The only thing akin to relief was being skin to skin with Jonas, was seeing with my own eyes that he was breathing. Seeing him safe.

But this was Edgewood. *Of course* he was safe. We all were.

I squeezed the bare skin on Blossom's soft arm, just to stay grounded.

"Sorry," I said. "I'm just—" I searched for a good excuse, but I didn't have one.

"Some town steward you'll be." The spite in Arrow's voice alarmed me.

"*Arrow*," Blossom hissed. She squeezed my arm back.

"What? It's like we can't say anything to her anymore," Arrow said.

I winced, but he was right. My family had been treating me with kid gloves for months. They sensed that I was off but couldn't articulate why. And how could I blame them? It's not as though I'd volunteered information. How could I? Mental illness didn't happen in Edgewood, wasn't something anyone in our town had ever needed to support their loved ones in. They were out of practice. They'd never been *in* practice.

I barely understood it myself, had no idea what was happening to me until Charlie's mother recognized the signs. She had postpartum anxiety with both her children and had quietly mentored me through it, respecting my requests for privacy. I didn't want my family to suspect my brokenness.

Arrow had always resented me for being the oldest, as if that's something I could help. He's only two years younger than me, but in his view, he was born three years too late. He would never be town steward and it grated on him.

"But I'm the oldest *boy*," he used to tell my mother, which always earned him a sharp glare.

"You know that's not how it works," she would tell him sharply. "Gender has nothing to do with it. Faye is the firstborn."

Except it wasn't untrue, not entirely. I was not the firstborn child of this family: the true firstborn was no longer alive. The thought made me flinch and mentally I flicked it away, a bug that buzzes with the endless hunger of the roaring darkness.

I didn't know all the details, just that my sister Autumn died before I was born. It was a truth I avoided looking at too closely, scared of what it could imply. If nothing bad was permitted to happen in Edgewood, how could an infant have died. The roar became louder. I didn't want to think about babies dying.

As town stewards, it was my family's job to nurture this town, ensure things ran smoothly, protect it. Keep it a safe haven.

With the hand not holding the popcorn, I touched the beaded Rowan necklace around my neck. The gesture was a habit. The necklace had been crafted for my older sister when she was born and gifted to me after her death. It made me feel close to her; I'd worn it for so long that the weight of it around my neck was as much a part of me as a limb. A book in my dad's study claimed that the wood of the Rowan tree was a guard against evil spirits and wicked enchantments. We weren't in need of any such charms in Edgewood—its very existence was a guard against all manner of evils—but still, it was a totem in its own right. A familiar, soothing comfort. Something solid for my fingers to cling to when the first terrible question raged, followed—always—by the one that was quieter, and worse.

What happened to Autumn?

(*And can it happen to my son?*)

CPSIA information can be obtained
at www.ICGtesting.com
Printed in the USA
LVHW101954161121
703501LV00020B/483

9 781943 720675